Days of Innocence

OTHER LOTUS TITLES

Anil Dharker	*Icons: Men & Women Who Shaped Today's India*
Aitzaz Ahsan	*The Indus Saga: The Making of Pakistan*
Ajay Mansingh	*Firaq Gorakhpuri: The Poet of Pain & Ecstasy*
Alam Srinivas	*Women of Vision: Nine Business Leaders in Conversation*
Amarinder Singh	*The Last Sunset: The Rise & Fall of the Lahore Durbar*
Aruna Roy	*The RTI Story: Power to the People*
Ashis Ray	*Laid to Rest: The Controversy of Subhas Chandra Bose's Death*
Bertil Falk	*Feroze: The Forgotten Gandhi*
Harinder Baweja (Ed.)	*26/11 Mumbai Attacked*
Harinder Baweja	*A Soldier's Diary: Kargil – The Inside Story*
Ian H. Magedera	*Indian Videshinis: European Women in India*
Kunal Purandare	*Ramakant Achrekar: A Biography*
Lucy Peck	*Agra: The Architectural Heritage*
Lucy Peck	*Delhi a Thousand Years of Building: An INTACH-Roli Guide*
M.J. Akbar	*Blood Brothers: A Family Saga*
Maj. Gen. Ian Cardozo	*Param Vir: Our Heroes in Battle*
Maj. Gen. Ian Cardozo	*The Sinking of INS Khukri: What Happened in 1971*
Madhu Trehan	*Tehelka as Metaphor*
Manish Pachouly	*The Sheena Bora Case*
Moin Mir	*Surat: Fall of A Port Rise of A Prince Defeat of the East India Company in the House Of Commons*
Monisha Rajesh	*Around India in 80 Trains*
Noorul Hasan	*Meena Kumari: The Poet*
Prateep K. Lahiri	*A Tide in the Affairs of Men: A Public Servant Remembers*
Rajika Bhandari	*The Raj on the Move: Story of the Dak Bungalow*
Ralph Russell	*The Famous Ghalib: The Sound of my Moving Pen*
Rahul Bedi	*The Last Word: Obituaries of 100 Indian who Led Unusual Lives*
R.V. Smith	*Delhi: Unknown Tales of a City*
Salman Akthar	*The Book of Emotions*
Sharmishta Gooptu	*Bengali Cinema: An Other Nation*
Shrabani Basu	*Spy Princess: The Life of Noor Inayat Khan*
Shahrayar Khan	*Bhopal Connections: Vignettes of Royal Rule*
Shantanu Guha Ray	*Mahi: The Story Of India's Most Successful Captain*
S. Hussain Zaidi	*Dongri to Dubai*
Sunil Raman & Rohit Aggarwal	*Delhi Durbar: 1911 The Complete Story*
Thomas Weber	*Going Native: Gandhi's Relationship with Western Women*
Thomas Weber	*Gandhi at First Sight*
Vaibhav Purandare	*Sachin Tendulkar: A definitive biography*
Vappala Balachandran	*A Life In Shadow: The Secret Story of ACN Nambiar – A Forgotten Anti-Colonial Warrior*
Vir Sanghvi	*Men of Steel: India's Business Leaders in Candid Conversation*

FORTHCOMING TITLE

M.S. Kohli	*A Life Full of Adventure: Leader of India's Epic Ascent of Everest in 1962*

Days of Innocence
Stories for Ruskin Bond

WRITERS' RETREAT I
Landour Mussoorie

Bulbul Sharma
Madhu Tandan
Ravi Shankar
Manju Kak
Binoo K. John
Pavan K. Varma
R.W. Desai
Namita Gokhale
Keki N. Daruwalla
Kanika Gahlaut
Sunny Singh
Pramod Kapoor

Photographs:
Harmit Singh

Namita Gokhale Editions
Roli Books

Namita Gokhale Editions

This edition first published in 2002
Second impression, 2016
Namita Gokhale Editions
An imprint of
Roli Books Pvt Ltd
M-75, G.K. II Market
New Delhi 110 048
Phone: 4068 2000
E-mail: info@rolibooks.com
Also at
Bengaluru, Chennai & Mumbai

Cover Design: Sneha Pamneja

ISBN: 978-81-7436-199-8

Typeset in Minion by Roli Books Pvt Ltd and printed at Repro India Ltd., Mumbai.

DEDICATION

The stories in this collection are dedicated to Ruskin Bond, who has resisted growing up for very many years. They are a collective tribute from all of us at the Retreat to his narrative genius, and to the undergrown or overgrown child within all of us.

Namita Gokhale, whose brainchild the Retreat was, watches an animated discussion with amusement. Bulbul seems to be lost in her own thoughts, while Manju waits her turn patiently.

Contents

AUTHORS AT THE RETREAT

BULBUL SHARMA

A painter and writer, Bulbul Sharma wrote a novel, *Banana Flower Dreams* in 1999 (Penguin) and has three collections of short stories to her credit: *My Sainted Aunts* (Harper Collins, 1992), *The Perfect Women* (UBS, 1994), and *Anger of the Aubergine* (Kali for Women, 1997). She is predominantly concerned with the changing pattern of Indian family life in her stories. She also works as an art teacher for mentally challenged children in Delhi. She played the art teacher at Mussoorie for a day, allowing the workshop participants to get in touch with their artistic side. Result: everybody discovered a few special shapes no one else had a clue about!

MADHU TANDAN

Madhu Tandan and her husband chose to abandon a comfortable city life to join a small self-sufficient community in the Himalaya where they spent seven years. This experience inspired Madhu's first novel, *Faith and Fire. A Way Within*

(Harper Collins, 1997). The writer has also worked with the World Wildlife Fund, India; Spastic Society of India, and the environment group formed by the late Kamala Devi Chattopadhyay at the India International Centre. Researching on dreams for many years, she is completing her second book, *A Dialogue with Dreams* (Harper Collins), based on the life stories of people she has met. At the Retreat, Madhu took people by the hand into the surreal territory of dreams when she conducted a dream analysis session around a bonfire and under the stars. Soon, she was everybody's Dream Girl!

RAVI SHANKAR
He published his first fiction work, in his mother tongue Malayalam, when he was a 15-year-old student. His next work, *Scream of the Dragonflies* (Harper Collins), a best-selling collection of short stories, came out in 1996. In between, the author worked as a political cartoonist with the *Indian Express* and became the art director of a media group. A man of many roles, he was also Deputy Editor of *India Today*, its art director and columnist. His novel, *The Tiger by the River*, was published in 2002. His pony-tailed presence, prodigious wit and bonfire jokes (all unprintable – unlike his work) are often remembered by Retreat participants with a gleam in their eyes.

MANJU KAK
Manju Kak started off as a painter and teacher in the eighties. She turned to writing and her labours were rewarded in 1990, when she won a short story award sponsored by Hongkong University and the British Council. Four years later she had published *First Light in Colonelpura* (Penguin) and then the short story, *Requiem for an Unsung Revolutionary* (Ravi Dayal, 1996). In between, she was awarded the Charles Wallace Fellowship for Creative Writing. She has pursued an interest in the Kumaon Himalaya for the last many years and one of her continuing concerns has been women's empowerment. At the

Retreat, Manju was the quintessential feminist, attacking weaknesses and thrusting for points during spirited discussions.

BINOO K. JOHN
A freelance journalist and writer, Binoo K. John has written on a variety of subjects. His quiet presence at the Retreat, interspersed by an off-and-on subtle sense of humour, made him a 'nice guy to have around'.

PAVAN K. VARMA
A versatile and multi-faceted personality, Pavan K. Varma joined the Indian Administrative Service in 1976. His major interest is poetry and it is reflected in the books he has done on and for poets. *Ghalib: The Man and Times* was followed by translations of the poetry of Kaifi Azmi and of Prime Minister Atal Behari Vajpayee's *21 Poems.* He has himself written *Draupadi and Yudhishtra*, a long work in verse. Pavan combines a flair for poetry with a keen eye for social analysis, best seen in the seminal and well-received *The Great Indian Middle Class.* The talents made him adjudicator of most of the bonfire sessions at the Writers' Retreat. Along with his charming wife Renu, he was ever the diplomat, always orderly – amid a bohemian group – in word and dress.

R.W. DESAI
Rupin Desai, retired professor of English at the University of Delhi, is the author of *Yeats's Shakespeare* (Northwestern University Press, 1971); *Sir John Falstaff, Knight* (Westburg Associates, 1974); a novel of ideas, *Frailty they name is WOMAN* (Har-Anand, 1993); and a collection of short stories, *Of War and War's Alarums and 21 other stories* (Writers' Workshop, 1998). He edits *Hamlet Studies*, an international journal of research exclusively on Shakespeare's *Hamlet.* The spirit of *Hamlet* never strays far from him and how could the Retreat have been an exception? Dogged by the ghost of the play

himself, the good professor could not fail to organise a rendition of *Hamlet's* opening scene.

NAMITA GOKHALE

Namita Gokhale was born in Lucknow in 1956. Her first novel, *Paro, Dreams of Passion*, was published to widespread acclaim in 1984. Her other books include *Gods, Graves, and Grandmother* (1994), *A Himalayan Love Story* (1996), *Mountain Echoes* (1998), *The Book of Shadows* (1999), and *The Book of Shiva* (2001). Namita is also a columnist and writes and reviews for several prominent newspapers and magazines. She publishes a signature imprint, Namita Gokhale Editions, in collaboration with Roli Books. She was responsible for everything organisational at the Retreat and was seen constantly gathering, disbanding, encouraging, and moving on her flock – the perfect Good Shepherdess.

KEKI N. DARUWALLA

One of India's foremost poets, Keki Daruwalla has published 12 volumes of poetry. He was awarded the Sahitya Akademi Award in 1984 for *The Keeper of the Dead*, an anthology of poetry, and won the Commonwealth Poetry Award for Asia in 1987 for *Landscapes*, another collection of poems. He has written two volumes of fiction. The latest, *The Minister for Permanent Unrest*, incorporates 17 short stories and one novella. He has also written extensively on international issues for the *Economic Times* from 1990 to 1995 and for *Hindustan Times*. He has been reviewing poetry for the last three decades. Our very own Bard at the Writers' Retreat, he summed up the experience thus:

Thoughts open up like parachutes
And drift away, as if a strong wind
Has carried them into the woods.
(From the poem, *Chillum*)

KANIKA GAHLAUT

Kanika Gahlaut is a journalist of long standing. She has worked with *First City*, *Sun*, the *Asian Age*, launching the magazine edition of the news daily in London and the *Indian Express*. Features are her forte and she is constantly focused on 'high' life for stewarding the much-maligned and much-read Page Three of the newspaper of today. For Kanika Gahlaut this means partying is work. Landour and Mussoorie presented no problem in this regard: she simply carried on from where she had left partying in Delhi. Her enthusiasm and *bindaas* manner added to the spirit (generously imbibed) of the workshop.

SUNNY SINGH

Sunny Singh has worked as a journalist, teacher, and as a management executive for multinationals in Mexico, Chile, and South Africa. She has been writing on a full-time basis for the last many years. Also a playwright, her first play was *Birthing Athena*, which focused on evolving relationships and the price of ambition in post-liberalisation India. Her first novel, *Nani's Book of Suicides* (Harper Collins), was followed by the well-received, *Single in the City: The Independent Woman's Handbook* and *With Krishna's Eyes*. Sunny Singh was born in Benares and lives in London. A voluble and lively participant at the Retreat, her joie de vivre was as infectious as her spirit of camaraderie.

PRAMOD KAPOOR

Pramod Kapoor, publisher of Roli Books, donned the role of author at the Retreat too. A long-time love affair with books, no doubt, enthused his creative writing skills, turning them into print.

HARMIT SINGH

Harmit Singh, a Paris-based photographer, was as well read and well informed about the publishing world, as the authors present. Harmit was at the Retreat, doing what he does best –

photographing people, places, and cameos. His international fame is apparent in the photographs in the book.

RUSKIN BOND
Ruskin Bond was born in Himachal Pradesh but lives in Mussoorie. He was educated in Shimla and became a professional writer at a young age. He needs no introduction: for an entire generation of readers he is a much-beloved writer of stories combining old-fashioned charm and gentleness with neat plots and the easily identifiable atmosphere of a bygone era. His acclaimed novel is *Room on the Roof* and his short story, *A Flight of Pigeons,* was made into the film, *Junoon.* Ruskin, the centre-point of the Writers' Retreat, the archetypal man of the mountains, invoked the nostalgia he is so famous for by taking the group on a memorable walk to a Landour cemetery and regaling them with ghost stories and jokes.

INTRODUCTION

Namita Gokhale

Writers are generally, in the popular imagination, considered to be different from the ordinary run of people, and by the dozen, this condition presumably stands multiplied. Yet, in late March 2001, when Namita Gokhale Editions and Roli Books decided to host a Writers' Retreat in Mussoorie and Landour, we found ourselves in the midst of a spontaneous out-pouring of creativity and camaraderie. A community of ideas sounds like a splendidly impossible ideal, but most of us who gathered in the decrepit grandeur of the Savoy hotel in Mussoorie spent the next few days in connecting with each other and letting go of the practical dynamics of our daily lives.

The idea was to get a few writers and literary journalists to hang out together and see what came of it. The presiding genius of storytelling in our little group was Ruskin Bond, one of India's most eminent and beloved writers. Literature is writing that endures. Ruskin Bond's work has survived the vagaries of generations of readers. The simplicity, universality, and lack of pretension in his writings make them especially accessible to young minds. On personally encountering Bond, one is struck by his portly bearing, and there is a certain gravitas in the manner in which he conducts himself. However, if you look into his eyes, which are guarded by stern spectacles with thick lenses, you encounter a mischievous glint. A shy schoolboy grin lights up his face, and the famous charm and humour hits you full force. Ruskin is a fun person, a funny person, and spending a long weekend with him in Landour transported us collectively and individually to the days of innocence we all once knew.

So there we were, in the heart of Ruskin territory, watching the shadows of the deodars lengthen, even as the brittle night lights of tourist-town Mussoorie tried to evade the depth and gloom of the Himalayan nights. We were a varied bunch of people: an assortment of ages, sizes, and attitudes. Let me attempt some brief introductions:

There was Bulbul Sharma, the vivacious, effervescent writer and painter, who is so intensely committed to life and joy and living. Bulbul has written some very highly regarded fiction, notably *My Sainted Aunts*, *The Anger of the Aubergines* and *Banana Flower Dreams*. She also consumes her inexhaustible energies in working with deprived and disabled children, conducting regular art and writing workshops for them.

Then there was Madhu Tandan, whose first book, *Faith and Fire*, about her experiences in a Himalayan ashram, subjected religious life to rigorous self-examination. Madhu was, in those Mussoorie days, researching her forthcoming book on dream interpretation. On the very first evening of the Retreat, we assembled around a smoky fire in the hotel lawns to swap dreams and nightmares. Our friend Ravi Shankar insists that the ever-helpful waiters of the Savoy dismantled a few antique chairs and flung them into the bonfire, but then he is a very imaginative man! Writing and fictionalising as a creative condition can be comparable to controlled dreaming and for the duration of the retreat, Madhu become the recipient of everybody's dream queries and dream anxieties.

Ravi Shankar is the caustic pony-tailed journalist and cartoonist whose hallmark black humour illuminated his first book of short stories, *The Scream of the Dragonfly*. Ravi's first novel, *The Tiger by the River*, a poetic, allegorical and deeply moving account of three generations of royal hunters, is due for international publication soon.

Manju Kak has published two outstanding collections of short stories: *First Light in Colonelpura* and *Requiem for a Revolutionary*. Manju's acute intelligence combines with an abstracted absent-mindedness which is most endearing. She has spent much time in the Kumaon and Garhwal hills researching and documenting the lifestyles and artistic and craft traditions of the Uttaranchal hills.

Pavan K. Varma is the multifaceted writer and diplomat whose work includes definitive books on Ghalib and Lord Krishna. His book on *The Great Indian Middle Class* is a classic of sorts on contemporary India. He has translated the poems of Kaifi Azmi into English from the original Urdu, and is as prolific as he is brilliant. Pavan was accompanied by his pipe and his wife Renu, who radiates warmth and intelligence, and is famous in Delhi and capitals around the world for her incomparable hospitality.

Rupin W. Desai has been professor of English at Delhi University for more years than he or any of us can remember. He has published a novel, *Frailty thy Name is WOMAN* and a book of short stories, *Of War and War's Alarums*. However, he is best known for his journal on Hamlet studies, which he has single-handedly brought out and published for the last two decades. We spent a golden afternoon in Landour doing an impromptu contextual reading and interpretation of Hamlet, much more giggly and irreverent than this description might suggest.

Keki N. Daruwalla is one of India's most reputed poets,

and the long-standing secretary and father-figure of the Poetry Society of India. Keki has served as a senior bureaucrat to the government of India, and his book of short stories, *The Minister of Permanent Unrest* examines the contradictions of our society with wisdom and insight. Keki crafts his stories with the same meticulous precision with which he writes poetry, and his readings of both prose and poetry have resonance and depth. Keki and Rupin's late-night readings of Ruskin's stories had us all enthralled (except for the alcoholics by the bonfire who preferred melancholic Hindi film songs).

Kanika Gahlaut is the young, fashionable, and acerbic journalist from *The Indian Express* group, and the much-feared countess of the 'page three' celebrity circuit. Kanika has recently written a novel which I have been privileged to read in manuscript, and the short story she has written for this compilation is acutely moving in its simplicity and honesty.

Sunny Singh's first novel, *Nani's Book of Suicides*, is a multi-layered and enigmatic work. She has also written the book *The Single Woman's Guide to Survival.* Sunny is radically intuitive and very funny, and mixes exotic Mexican cocktails which many of us at the Retreat readily succumbed to.

Pramod Kapoor of Roli Books crossed over from the publisher/writer divide and penned an inscrutable and introspective story culled from childhood memories of an old *haveli* in Benares. We look forward to more creative writing from Pramod.

Ganesh Saili is an extraordinary writer, raconteur, and photographer – a presiding eminence of the Garhwal hills. Ganesh and Ruskin kept all of us entertained with mountain-tales, folklore, and a constant flow of jokes, ranging from brilliant to outrageous. These *creative* writers were the animals in the safari. The observers from the literary pages of the newspapers and magazines were equally special, stimulating, and involved. We are grateful to all of them for not blowing our collective *creative* cover.

Mini Kapoor's gentle presence, Sheela Reddy's perceptive insights, Anita Joshua's quiet attentiveness – all knit the writers and press together. Aditi Khanna's diaries brought the Retreat into the homes and active imaginations of innumerable readers. Tulika and her crew recorded our antics for digital posterity. Ratna Sahai and Veena Baswani minded and guided us, while Pramod and Kiran's inimitable hospitality made it all happen. Last, but of course not least, Harmit Singh, the peripatetic international photographer, documented our precious time together with a series of superlative photographs which have brought an element of timelessness to our fragile memories.

HIDING AWAY

Bulbul Sharma

The grass had changed from green to grey as dusk crept in quietly behind my back. I was hiding once again, this time behind the old gate, waiting for someone to come and find me or at least start looking for me. I hid from my family regularly in places that were secret but not so secret that none could find me. I had my favourite hiding places, which were scattered not very far from the house, safe places from where I could see the veranda and bits of the garden. I was about eight when I first began hiding and gradually, as I realised the heady feeling of creating alarm in others, forcing them to worry about me, I began to run away even more frequently. At first my mother, our old *ayah* and my sisters showed a satisfying, genuine fear when they found I was missing. They rushed around the house, shouting, 'Khuku, Bulbul, baby … Where are you?' Their voices laced with worry would reach me where I was hiding and my skin would prickle with joy. I loved the way they called out my various pet names; the high notes and the agitated voices gliding towards me filled me with happiness and reassurance. Then, one day, they lost interest. My cousin, who had just returned from the US, told my mother that I had an attention problem and that they should ignore me. 'She is nine years old, not a toddler with whom you have to play hide and seek all day,' said this cousin, who wore gold-rimmed glasses that glinted even in the dark, 'You spoil her, *kakima*,' he said, not looking at me.

'I do not spoil her. It's her father,' said my mother, and then they began talking about an English film, using words I could not understand. We were sitting in the veranda watching the fireflies, which had come out for the first time after the rains. The garden, with its stunted flowering trees looked bigger at night, making my secret hiding places darker and farther away from the house. I was not spoilt by anyone. They just felt sorry for me because I was not as cute and fair and plump as my brother. 'When both of you go out in the pram, people think you are my child, instead of *memsahib's*. Can't blame them, your skin is so dark,' said *Ayah* whom I called Sarla-ma. She made special sweets out of *gur* and coconut for my brother which none of us, except for my father, was allowed to taste. 'Open your mouth, my little Nandgopal, my piece of the moon,' she would say, and pop one glistening brown sweet into his mouth. My brother carried these sticky sweets in his pockets and then when Sarla-ma was not looking, he would give me one. But then she gave him some more sweets and made him swallow each one in front of her, coaxing him with soft words.

Everyone loved my brother, not just Sarla-ma. Even the beggar who came to the gate in the afternoons, crying out in a cheerful voice, 'Give us a coin, one coin for one old man.' He would look straight at my brother, blinking his yellow eyes. Sometimes we lobbed a coin at him, sending it high over the gate since we were not allowed to go out of the house alone. The beggar always jumped up and caught it deftly despite his lame leg. Then he would look at my brother, wink and smile before limping away, leaving a trail of dust. The beggar never asked me for anything and once, when I gave him a banana I had saved from lunch, he just slipped it into his large cloth bag and turned away.

The grass beneath my feet now looked like a black rug, with tufts of white gleaming where the street light fell. Maybe I should have hidden earlier, before the tailor had come. I could hear my mother's voice scolding him for making the sleeves of her blouse too tight. I stood on my toes and looked over the gate post. Sarla-ma was sitting on the steps of the veranda with a plate. Was she waiting for me? It was getting really dark outside now, much darker than it ever seemed from the house when I looked out of the window at night. The cement gate post I was leaning against felt cold against my back and when I rubbed my hand on it, the white chalk came off. I could see everything in the veranda clearly, now that they had switched all the lights on for the tailor to check the faults in Ma's misshapen blouse. It was as if I was in a theatre hall, watching a play. One by one they came out into the veranda – my brother, my sisters, my cousin with the glinting glasses – and stood around Ma. They held cups in their hands and my brother looked out into the lawn, pointing at something. Was it a firefly or was he looking for me?

The tailor, having accepted defeat, was preparing to leave. Now my mother would look around and see that I was not there. She would ask Sarla-ma where I was. Everyone would know that I was not there. Any minute now, they would begin rushing about, calling out for me. I waited, my legs sinking into the grass which seemed to get deeper. A pigeon fluttered on the broken ledge of the gate post, its wings grey and blurred. Yesterday, Mali had found a snake in the garden. He had killed it with the handle of the lawn-mower, shouting at us not look into the dead snake's eyes. 'It will remember who killed it and come back for them later, when it is born again in another life.'

How long is another life? Why don't they ask for me? 'See Ma, I'm here. I am hiding here.' I tried to shout, but my voice was stuck in my throat. The gate post pushed against me, cold and white, making me sink into the grass. The darkness gathered around me tightly and I felt I could not breathe. Waves of fear and panic rose in my body, holding me down as I tried to move towards the house. Then everything – the house, the garden, the brightly lit veranda – everything disappeared. My hand, which I held in front of my face, was a line of black. We were all lost, each one of us, as I had seen before in so many nightmares. I would never find them again because they would not know who I was anymore. I could search forever but never find my family, my house, the arid garden, the veranda with five cane chairs, the steps where Honey's pups were born last week, the sandboxes with the footprints of a thief who stole my mother's gold necklaces. I tried again to call out to Ma, to my brother, to my sisters, but I could not remember who they were. Fear flooded over me and I could not remember my own name.

'Bull, bullooo ... Khukoo,' sang the sweet voice from behind a beam of light. I ran towards it, suddenly free of the darkness. My father stopped the car at the gate and called out again. 'What are you doing here in the dark, you silly girl?' he said, scolding me in his soft, tired voice as I held his hand. The house was lit with candles and my mother came down the steps, her sari *pallav* floating behind her like an angel's wings. 'The lights have gone off again. Why are you roaming about in the dark? Had your milk, Bulbul?' she asked absent-mindedly, patting my head. I still held my father's hand but not so tightly now. The fear ebbed away, leaving no traces. I had forgotten the darkness, though the garden was a sheet of glistening black shadows now. It was as if I had never been afraid, never felt the cold despair that had wrapped itself around me just a few minutes before. My father let go of my hand but I could still stand. When he died eleven years later, I reached too late to see him, to hold his hand – to thank him for finding me even though he did not know I was lost. After that day, I never went into hiding again. Instead, I found new ways to seek attention but a fear of darkness, of being alone, still shadows me.

THE SANCTUARY

Madhu Tandan

'There is a tumour in the upper intestine. I've done a needle biopsy. We should know the result in three days,' my doctor told me as I lay in the recovery room.

I was stunned that my body had turned traitor and was harbouring a tumour. I was only forty-seven, too young to be reminded that death was a possibility.

'Is it malignant?' I whispered as if sharing a dark secret.

'The biopsy report will tell us what we are up against,' the doctor said.

The pain had first hit me at night when I had felt as though a pair of hands was tearing my stomach apart. Vijay had awoken with my cry and given me a painkiller. When the incident recurred two days later, investigations were inevitable. Probes and scopes and half a day of tests could only be measured by two emotions – hope and despair. Throughout, I had hoped it was just an infection and despaired of any thought that took me further. Now my mind felt defenceless against the truth.

It could be benign, but if it isn't … was all the elasticity my thoughts permitted me as I came home. When Vijay reassuringly held my hand and said, 'I'm sure everything will be alright,' I did not hear conviction in his voice, but fear.

I could not be dying, I thought as I lay in bed that night, and sadness overwhelmed me. I have too much to do. My thoughts rushed and pooled with worry around Karuna who, at twenty-six, was still not married. How adamant Karuna had been when she was twenty-two.

'I have better things to do than get married and if ever I do, I must first fall in love with the man I marry. Get to know him …'

The *better things* slowly began to vanish. Karuna's job became monotonous and the years flew by with her heart still intact.

How many prospective bridegrooms and their families I had called over, answering their repetitive questions. Yet the ones with promise seemed to get fixed up elsewhere, and slowly anxiety gripped me. I wondered how much time I had left to see her settled.

And how would my Vijay manage? He – who, when we had first met – felt he could not keep his eyes off me! Why then, after our marriage, were we like two porcupines huddling together for warmth on a cold winter's night? If we came too close, our quills pricked one another, and when we moved apart we longed for the warmth of closeness. In between these two spaces, our lives shuffled.

Over time, the quills did not hurt as much and the warmth had grown, so that now regret filled me for all the years that could have been lived differently.

Why am I overcome with this absurd notion that my life could have been different? Though I'm not sure how, and in what way. I feel like a mist-dweller who has walked the miles and years of life seeking some unknown, imperishable star. And was I able to find it? I think not. Neither in my vanities and triumphs, nor in my tryst with sorrow, as though the price we pay for living is to lose its intangible essence. Yet my sleepless eyes had kept their vigil, asking for the impossible – a sense of completion through life's partial joys and relative sorrows.

I searched for it in every coming event, in each new experience, hoping that the ensuing wave would lift its deep-sea treasures to the shore. But every time, there was something missing. It fell short of an ancient dream imprinted on my heart of an inviolate sanctuary I had still to find.

And now, more than ever before, the silence of the night asked me: Where from? Where to? Whatever for? Was that all there was to my life – an incomplete poem, a knotted handkerchief as a reminder of a forgotten promise and marks on a page where the ink had run out?

Nothing answered, except the wetness of tears as sleep overtook me. I had a strange dream that night:

I am walking through a forest and chance upon a clearing where sunlight filters through the trees to collect in a circle on the ground, like a spotlight on a stage. Illumined in this light is a dancing deer! I watch fascinated as he pirouettes, keeping in time with music only he can hear. His golden coat shines in the sun, investing form with beauty, grace with abandon. The deer appears to have found something so precious that he can only dance to celebrate his moment of freedom.

Sometimes there is an eloquence to dreams that real life can never match. I saw boneless fluidity dance with sheer joy, seemingly emanating from some secret mysterious fount, so that the deer was imbued with a strange, magical power.

I awoke from the dream, enclosed in a halo of quietude. Why did I feel that I was being given a clue, a hint to my enigma? I closed my eyes to recapture the enchantment of the dancing deer. Was it telling me that my health would return and that the dance of life would continue with all its former abandon? My despair needed hope, like hunger demanding appeasement; yet another part of my mind observed that there was something distinctly familiar about the deer. He had looked at me with eyes that were greeting an old friend, asking me to remember what I had forgotten.

My breath caught the moment I remembered. The deer was Kundan, my childhood companion and the keeper of my soul. The amnesia of childhood cleared, like the mist on the sunlight of remembrance. I was that six-year-old child again, staying with my parents in a huge cantonment bungalow, which had high ceilings and cool floors. There was a sprawling garden in front and a large compound at the back, which seemed to merge with the forest behind, even though there was a fence to remind us of boundaries.

It was in this compound that I spent most of my time, for there we had a pet peacock, two cows which lived under an open shed amidst an army of squirrels scurrying up and down trees, and of course, Toofan, my irrepressible cocker spaniel.

This rather easy atmosphere suddenly became charged one evening when a *jawan* arrived with something in his arms. He saluted my father and set down what he was carrying. When I looked closely I was amazed. It was a baby deer! The *jawan* said that its mother had died and he had found him alone and defenceless in the jungle. We were all standing watching when suddenly the deer tried to bolt. After a few frantic moments of running around blindly, he stood quietly behind the protection of a pillar, his black eyes scared and ready for flight.

The deer instantly enchanted me. I loved animals, but he was different. He seemed to me like a mysterious creature that had arrived from another land with his golden fur, stamped with coin-shaped white spots that trembled as he stood there. Seeing my excitement, my parents agreed to keep him.

Kundan was kept that night in an empty room at the back of the house. My mother could hardly get me to sleep as I jumped up and down on the bed and said, 'Suppose this deer has wings, then he will fly away at night.'

'We've bolted the door, so he cannot go away,' my mother said.

'But he is a fairy-deer and may disappear, and then I'll never see him again.'

'I promise you, if you go to sleep, he will be there in the morning.'

Barely had morning come, I dragged my mother to open the room where Kundan had spent the night. I heaved a sigh of relief when he leapt up and watched us warily. The bowl of milk we had left for him had remained untouched. In that moment, I was convinced that he was a deer with special powers, since he needed neither food nor water.

The days that followed saw Kundan become my constant companion as I fed, stroked, and talked to him. He wove his way into my imagination. When my mother told me a story about a faraway castle, I flew towards it on Kundan's back, while he named all the stars we passed en route. He slew the wicked monsters of the night that visit children in their dreams, by saying the magic words that turned them into stone. As the months passed, Kundan became my guardian from the other world – a world where we do brave and beautiful things in strange and bewitching lands. But why did it all fade away, as did Kundan?

One day, a year after Kundan's arrival, the inevitable happened. I had just stepped out into the back veranda, when I saw him bounding towards the fence. In one clean jump, he scaled it and disappeared into the forest. Till today, I remember the sun shining on his back as he leapt to freedom. I knew, with the instinct of a child, that I would never see him again. I mourned his loss, and soon after, fell ill asking the one question I needed an answer to – where has Kundan gone?

Yes, where had Kundan gone, the adult in me asked? Where has that child gone who felt the magic of the world and watched everything unfold in wonder? When did my palate become so jaded by habit, inundated by trivia, so lost in the avalanche of daily worries, that I had forgotten I once owned a magical deer? A deer who had whispered to me secrets of the universe, which had made my young heart swell with pride to belong to such a world.

An odd restlessness overtook me. I got out of bed and sat on the terrace waiting for dawn to break over the city. I knew there was something else that was attached to Kundan's leaving, a memory that suddenly seemed very important to recall. In it lay the clue to understanding this hollow feeling in my heart that was suddenly questioning everything, and yet looking for a refuge.

My mother had told me the story of where Kundan had gone, when I had questioned her more than once. I do not know whether she had heard this story from her mother, or made it up, but as I look back, it had an uncanny resemblance to how my life unfolded later. Was she instinctively warning me, preparing me by telling me what to expect?

'Kundan jumped the fence because he was searching for something,' my mother had told me.

'What was he searching for?' I had asked.

'He himself did not know. Something outside the compound was calling him.'

'Where did he go?'

After jumping the fence, he found a hillside of sweet smelling roses, marigolds, flaming red poppies, and wild daisies that warmed his heart with their beauty. He smelt some, nibbled at others, quite happy where he was, when suddenly he saw a herd of deer coming towards him. The leader of the herd said, 'You cannot stay here. This is a special area, which you can only look at from afar. You must come with us.'

'Where are you going?' Kundan asked.

'There is a carnival on the other side of the mountain. A huge market place is set up, where hundreds of deer will arrive from all over. There, the fast runners are separated from the slower ones, those with brighter coats from the duller ones, and the deer with a sharper sense of smell from those with less.'

'But why must I go to the market place?' Kundan asked.

'Everyone must join the market place at some point or the other, for there you find out what kind of deer you are.'

So Kundan joined the herd. They went through glades and meadows, where more deer joined them. During the journey, Kundan realised that some deer ran ahead, while the slower ones were always looking longingly at those that ran fast.

'Where was Kundan?'

'He always kept on the fringe of the group, because that gave him the freedom to wander slightly away from the herd without actually straying completely.'

After many days, Kundan and the herd reached a lake around which they rested. Then they entered a forest, which was so thick that no light penetrated the canopy of trees, and the dense foliage hampered their progress. Suddenly they heard the rasping cough of a leopard and realised they were in danger. The leader counted the herd, but already two were missing. The deer stamped their feet nervously and looked over their shoulders constantly, anxious about the darkness and what lay beyond.

One of the deer said, 'My grandfather warned me about this forest. It is full of leopards. A one-eyed giant also lives here, who can enslave us. He also said that if we reached the ridge of the mountain in front, then we would be safe.'

By now, Kundan's heart was pounding. He jumped over the foliage, wove his way across the trees; sometimes hiding, sometimes running, never knowing when the forest would end, unsure where the one-eyed monster, or a leopard, was lurking.

Finally, the forest cleared and they moved towards the ridge of the mountain where they lay down exhausted but relieved.

When morning came, they went down the other side of the ridge, which was bare of trees and greenery. They entered the valley below, only to discover to their horror, a marshland

– brown, squelchy, bubbling with greed to consume anyone who dared cross it. The deer could not turn back because they wanted to reach the market place, but how were they going to cross the marshland?

There was a delighted cry from one of the deer who pointed to some plants in the marshes that were different to the main bulk. There were small tufts of these, like islets, big enough for one hoof to step on. They were scattered all over the marshland, till as far as the eye could see.

Hope surged in all of them as they prodded one of the tufts and it felt firm. 'I'll try it first,' a deer said bravely and stepped on the tufts. Everyone cheered with enthusiasm but that feeling soon turned to dismay. The deer had barely covered a little distance when his feet sank and the marsh gobbled him up.

Tears poured down Kundan's cheeks. All the deer grew sad, while they sat beside the marsh and contemplated their fate.

Three days and three nights passed before Kundan rose and said, 'I'm going to try and cross this marsh. But I'm going to do it in a different way.'

He lightly put his hoof on the first islet, but did not let his full weight settle on it before he skipped onto the next and the next, barely touching the tufts with feather-like lightness. To the utter amazement of the herd, Kundan crossed the marsh.

In my youth, I too had begun my journey unafraid to hope, to yearn, to dream. The hillside of flowers that Kundan smelt and nibbled, after he jumped the fence, were my days of idealism, when I thought of disentangling the world-skein to weave from it a carpet of perfection. But soon enough I was herded in search of the market place, to discover what kind of deer I was.

I joined an advertising agency, produced mediocre copy; moved to a cultural centre, where amidst theatre artists, singers and dancers, I came into my own as their coordinator. Like Kundan, I seemed to stay at the edge of the herd, not completely mainstream, especially in the kind of work I chose. And did I find out how fast I could run, or how bright my coat was? Yes and No. For can anyone really judge himself or herself objectively, besides hoping that one is more than what one actually is, and fearing that one is less than that.

From watching others perform on stage, I was cast in my own real-life role. Events went into fast-forward: I married Vijay; a year later his recently widowed mother began to stay with us. She was an unhappy woman who constantly complained about how everything had been taken away from her – her husband, her house, how no one came to visit her, how bad her arthritis was, how useless the servants were, and how I never cooked the way she did.

Just when I was steeling myself to survive this psychic din, I became pregnant. Our tiny flat, my constant nausea, my mother-in-law's obsession with food, Vijay's growing work involvements, made me sick at heart. The forest Kundan passed through was truly dark and the leopards were devouring all I had hoped my life would be. My youthful idealism seemed lost in the avalanche of daily worries, where I was substituting habit for thought, and the one-eyed giant of self-pity was all but ready to enslave me.

Perhaps it was Karuna's birth, where my whole being had a new focus, that began my walk out of the forest. I climbed the ridge to safety on the back of motherhood.

And now, I am confronted with my own marshland. I have no idea whether I will be permitted to cross it or not.

Kundan had not stopped after he had crossed the marshland. He had gone on, but where and towards what? I gazed into the hourglass of memory and realised that the grains of sand revealed an infinitely precious pattern, which remained obscured till the moment was ripe. Was I now being permitted the access of remembrance to find a shelter after a long journey?

More than forty years ago, on a dark, moonless night, I had asked my mother, 'What happened to Kundan after he crossed the marshland?'

She had looked at me with pensive eyes and continued:

'He rested for a while, after his exertion of crossing the marshland. Just when he closed his eyes something odd happened.'

'What?' I had asked, eagerly.

The most beautiful scent wafted through the air, filling Kundan's nostrils with its gentle, overwhelming fragrance. He opened his eyes and looked around to see where it was coming from. He moved towards a clump of trees thinking it was coming from there. But no, it was not. So he moved towards the mountains, only to realise that the scent had no particular direction. It filled the entire air. He stood puzzled, not knowing which way to go, when out of the blue a man appeared. He wore a long robe and his grey hair was shoulder length, while his eyes were like two pools of light. In his hand he carried a lantern.

Instinctively, Kundan bowed his head with respect and asked, 'Sir, where does this beautiful scent come from?'

'It comes from the Sanctuary.'

'Sanctuary? Which Sanctuary?'

The man pointed in the direction of the evening sky, orange with the glow of the setting sun and said, 'Where the sky and Earth meet, where day turns to night, where spring turns to summer, and joy to sorrow – in the gap between the two – is the gateway to the Sanctuary. Beyond that is a magnificent mountain covered with silver snow, surrounded by a collar of gold. There you will find the most exquisite garden, where every flower and fruit that exists in the market place blooms at the same time. The fruits drip with juice, the crowns on the brows of the narcissi are bathed in gold, while the vapours rise to make a bed of water-lilies drunk with perfume as they serenade the roses. This garden is always in full bloom and no flower or fruit ever dies, so that the essence of their combined perfume is wafting down, drawing you towards it.'

'Have you been there, Sir?' Kundan asked.

'I live there, but I came down because I knew you were ready to hear of the Sanctuary.'

'All this while, I was in search of the market place. Where is that?'

The man laughed, 'When you jumped the fence and entered the valley of flowers, that was the market place. When you were trapped in the forest and despaired in the marshland, that too was the market place. When you crossed the marshland and rested, that was the market place as well.'

'How puzzling! You mean that all this while, when I was searching for the market place, I was in it?'

The man with the lantern nodded his head.

'Is the Sanctuary also the market place?' Kundan asked.

'The Sanctuary is the heart of the market place, yet beyond it.'

'But how did you know about all that I have been through?'

'Because I was there every step of the way,' the man answered.

'I did not see you.'

'You were too busy searching for the market place.'

'How come I see you now?'

'Because for the first time you have smelt the fragrance of the Sanctuary.'

Kundan grew quiet for a while, then raised his head and asked, 'Is it possible for me to go there?'

'I hope you will.'

'But how will I find it?'

'You have felt the yearning, now follow it. Trust the pull of the Sanctuary for it will protect you till you reach it.'

At this point, I had interrupted my mother and said, 'Mom, I too want to go to the Sanctuary.'

She had kept silent for a long while before replying, 'Unlike Kundan, you can take another way. Far away, you will find a small railway station where only one train comes at an unknown hour. It's a train you must not miss, because it can take you to the point where the earth and the sky meet. After that Kundan will be there to receive you.'

'Will you come with me to meet Kundan?' I had asked.

'I'll come with you ... I'll always be there as you search for your Kundan and your sanctuary.'

My mother was lost in thought, so I had pulled her arm and asked, 'How will I know when the train will come?'

'You will know, because the bells announcing this train will first ring in your heart. You must listen carefully so that you do not miss them. Then go straight to the station and you will find the train there.'

I was moved by the memory of the story, moved by a mother who had tried to give me the gift of *something more*, by asking me to listen to it, read its signs, heed its warnings.

Till now I had forgotten, and only a tumour growing in my body and the dream of Kundan dancing reminded me how far away I was from my sanctuary.

Dawn had broken over the city when Vijay joined me on the terrace. 'You're up early.'

'I awoke because I had a beautiful dream.'

'Was it telling you that all would be well?'

'That I do not know, but it reminded me of a vision I had lost.'

Two days later I went to the doctor to collect my report. My hands were clammy as I waited outside, my body tight with tension.

'It's benign,' the doctor said smiling, handing me the report to read with my own eyes.

Life, relief, hope surged through my veins like warm brandy, and my mind ran ahead of me. We'll have a party; we'll call

all our friends over; I must get new upholstery for the sofa; when can I fit in the operation? I hope I will be well enough for ... and before I knew it, I was back in the carnival of life.

Not quite. It was at dusk, the point between day and night, where illness had turned to health, and the earth meets the sky that I remembered again. Without knowing how, I had picked up an unknown rhythm that pulsates in the pause between two experiences, in the gap between waiting and finding, meetings and partings. I stood on my terrace, watching the city lights beam bright with energy, while a strange stillness swept through me: my body was completely relaxed, my mind like a pool without a ripple.

That night I had a dream, which till today, moves me when I think of it:

I'm sitting on an armchair in my room, when it suddenly turns into a bench on a deserted railway platform. I see a man approaching me from far away and as he comes nearer, I realise he has a lantern in his hand.

'This time I intend to catch the train,' I tell him.

'I know,' he says gently. 'I wanted to be there when you began your journey, and I will be there when you complete it.'

'And what happens, in between?'

'The scent will carry you home.'

And I believed him, for his eyes held a light that would never fade.

THE GHOSTMAKERS

Ravi Shankar

The blind man turns the corner, probing the space in front with a walnut cane which has a brass handle shaped like a Chinese dragon. It winks in the sun. His left hand is held straight to his side, the fist clenched tight as if he is holding an invisible dog on an invisible leash. He walks up the steps of the building, boot-heels clattering on the marble, and climbs up two flights of stairs. He turns left on a carpeted corridor which smells of air freshener and knocks on a door which says Dr Leena Seth, MD. He smiles, walks unerringly to the couch placed by the window and leans the cane against the wall. He looks out of the window, nods as if he sees something which satisfies him, and lies down. The doctor gets up from her chair and walks over to the high wing chair at the head of the couch. The blind man smiles. He does not take his dark glasses off. His face is long and smooth, clean shaven. He reaches out a hand and pats the air beside him.

'What is it that you did just now, Roshan?' Leena asks him.

'I petted Sirius,' he says. His voice is pleasant and husky.

'Who is Sirius?'

The man looks surprised. His fine eyebrows arch above the rims of his RayBans.

'My dog,' he says. Then he smiles. His teeth are even and white.

'Sorry Doctor,' the blind man says, 'I forgot you can't see.'

SESSION ONE

Doctor's notes: *Hypnotising the blind without a visual focus can be challenging. But using fragrances which are essentially soporofic like the smell of* raat-ki-raani *and* chameli, *incense of sandalwood and rose, the sound of water falling in the background – a simple fountain would suffice – or a pre-recorded tape of the sound of a river flowing, have been found useful as a background for suggestion. Certain musical instruments like the* veena, *sitar, and violin, along with a few esoteric Sanskrit* shlokas *also help induce a state of trance.*

The baby was born blind to this world. He was named Roshan. He had soft dark eyes which looked like grapefruit. He blinked a lot but when the doctor shone the flashlight into his eyes, the baby did not blink at all. His mother cried when she learnt that her son was blind. They therefore decided to name him Roshan. Roshan was a baby who smiled a lot. A quiet, inward smile. It dimpled his cheeks.

'He is smiling at the memories of his past birth,' his mother said to his father. His father sighed and stroked Roshan's hair. Roshan did not know that he was blind. When he opened his eyes, he saw the true nature of emptiness – it had no colour. But, beyond it, the world was dark and green, full of shadows. A tall man often came to stand by his cribside when he awoke, a tall man without eyes. His skin was stretched over his sockets, smooth and unlined. Next to him stood a pale woman with long hair the colour of weeds. Her hair was a mass of pleats among which grew black roses. The flowers were alive, their stems twisted among the weaves of her braid, their roots lost among the hair and disappearing into her scalp. Their garments were malachite and hung loose and free about them. The man smiled at Roshan and the woman leaned over him and crooned. Roshan gurgled happily and reached out to pluck a black rose from her hair.

'Look at him talk!' Roshan's mother said, 'My darling!'

'At least he isn't dumb,' his father muttered.

His mother threw a disapproving look at her husband and picked up the baby in her arms. The man and the woman stepped back, and started to fade away into the shadows in the distance. Roshan suddenly felt cold and alone. The shadows swallowed the black roses. He began to cry.

'Baby, baby,' his mother crooned. She was an invisible warmth which radiated from the emptiness around him as she held him to her breast. He touched her face, and his fingers came away wet. She put a warm, hard nipple into his crying mouth, squeezing her milk into his throat. Roshan did not stop his crying and kept turning his face away.

'The baby isn't feeding,' he heard his mother say. 'We've got to show him to the doctor.'

'He looks healthy enough,' Father's voice, thin and worried, 'yet he doesn't eat a thing.'

Roshan wasn't hungry; he had fed. When he was hungry, he did not cry. He looked at the green circle of the shadows far away and called in his throat. Across the empty space, the woman with the black roses would come, gliding in the air, her thin hands outstretched to stroke his cheek. Her hair would cloak his face and she would pluck the roses from her hair and squeeze their pulp and juices into his mouth. She sang to him a lullaby in a low sweet voice:

We are the Angels of Emptiness
We are the World-makers of the Sightless

We live in gardens full of black roses
We teach you how to cut your losses
Sleep soft, sleep low,
and you will dream what you will see ...
hush, baby, hush...

'Where is she now?' Leena's question.

The blind man looks at her as if he does not understand the question. Then he smiles.

'Sometimes I dream of her, but not always. But now, there are so many of us.'

His face softens, and he smiles to himself as if a lamp has been lit somewhere in the back room of a house. Then he gets up and clenches his fist, as if tightening an invisible leash. At the door, he turns towards Leena.

'Doctor Seth,' he calls softly. 'Your lipstick is all wrong.'

* * *

SESSION TWO

Doctor's notes: *The patient exhibits a marked imaginative streak, and is persuasively realistic about his fantasies. As if he wants everyone to believe in him. A need to possess what he cannot see seems to be at the root of his existence. But he is very functional and well balanced for someone so delusional. Multiple personality disorder co-existing with monomania? Compulsive obsessive?*

Two weeks later, he comes again, alone, punctual and without fuss. Most of Leena's patients are nervous before they settle into the couch, fidgeting and speaking fast. Some are sullen and hostile. Excavating minds makes for a strange job. But the blind man is smiling as he enters the room. His left hand is outstretched, fist tightly clenched. He suddenly falters, jerking forward as if he is being pulled.

'Sirius, behave yourself, sir!' he says sharply.

Then he stands straight again.

'He is a bit frisky today,' he apologises, patting the air beside him, 'it's the spring in the air.'

Leena raises her eyebrows. It is December.

'Tell me about Sirius,' she says.

It was when Roshan was three years old that he got a pup. He was a quiet child, who sat for most of the time in his baby rocking chair without rocking, gazing at the green shadows beyond the void. The void was like a circle of nothingness, fuzzy at the edges, and on its shore were the voluptuous gardens where the black roses grew. Every day, the pale woman came to him and he played with the dark roses in her hair and drank their dew. When his teeth began to appear, she would feed him the flowers without crushing them and they tasted sweet and fleshy. The man's visits became fewer, but he often accompanied the woman to the edge of the garden from where he stood and looked in Roshan's direction. When he learnt to walk, he tried to cross the empty space in front of him to reach the man but he always stumbled on something and fell. That was when he realised that the emptiness was full of things with blunt corners and sharp edges he could not see. He hurt himself and cried and his mother came running in from the kitchen. He always felt her approach through that empty space, a warm rush of fabric and scent, full of comfort and admonitions. Noises were always arising from the empty space, of things scraping and falling, footfalls and laughter.

Doors creaked open, windows slammed, automobiles honked and buzzed, engines clanked. It seemed as if the emptiness was full of loud ghosts who waylaid him whenever he tried to enter.

'Baby is lonely,' Mother told Father one evening. Roshan always wondered why his parents were the only human voices which inhabited his empty space, but became real only when he touched them. The next day, his father came into his room as he sat looking at the waterlights playing amongst the green shadows, waiting for the woman. Father crouched beside him and ruffled his hair. He smiled absently, hoping Father would go away. The woman never came when Father or Mother were around. Then Father thrust a soft and squirming bundle into his lap. It was warm, noisy, and scratchy. It smelt of milk and something furry. It licked Roshan's face and barked, trying to clamber over his chest. Roshan felt its warmth. He hugged it to his chest and smiled.

'Good, he likes the pup and it likes him too,' his father said. His mother laughed and patted him on his head.

'Now you have a friend,' his mother said, 'who will look after you.'

The pup, too, was something he could not see, but only smell and touch. But it kept him company all the time, never straying far from him, warming his sleep at night, licking him awake in the mornings. But whenever the woman came, it wailed and howled, refusing to come near.

'I want you to pet him,' he told her, 'I want you to feed him the black roses.'

The woman smiled sadly and stroked his hair.

'He doesn't like my roses,' she said. 'He is afraid of me.'

'But why?' Roshan asked. She did not answer.

'I want to see him,' Roshan pouted, 'and with him, I want to cross this emptiness and come visiting you and the skin-eyed man. I want to watch him play among the shadows and sleeping at night in your hair.'

She stroked his hair thoughtfully.

'You have to fill your emptiness yourself, child,' she said. 'Otherwise it will always be this way.'

'What do I fill it with?'

She leant across, kissing him on his brow with cool, dry lips.

'With life,' she answered.

Roshan did not understand. After she had gone, he sat

thinking for a long time. The emptiness throbbed and hummed. The puppy played beside him, a frisky, noisy presence full of warm slurpy licks and happy little yelps. Roshan wondered what life was. It was something he could not see. But he could hold it in his hands, feel its contours and inhale its smells. He picked up the puppy, a mass of fur from inside which came a steady, low thumping. He held it up to his ear, and he could feel something working inside the body of his puppy, which squirmed in his grasp. He heard a drumbeat which fed the emptiness, a liquid rush which cycled and coursed endlessly. He wanted it.

'I have to fill this emptiness with that drumbeat,' he said to himself. 'I must pour this hum into it and watch it spread.'

When night came and he lay in bed listening to the puppy's steady breathing, the woman came again. This time the man also stood beside her, his eyeless face looking down at him with a radiant love. The pup woke up with a bark, trying to jump down from the bed and run away. Roshan held it to him tight, and it howled and struggled. Roshan hugged it even tighter. His hands and face stung, his skin burned. Then the pup gave a frantic kick and slumped in his hands. In the void before him, he saw a small shape beginning to form. First, he saw a white star. Then a forehead, and intelligent, inquiring brown eyes. Then a long face with a pink tongue. It looked at Roshan with its head cocked to one side, tail wagging. Then it got up and pranced around him, inviting him to get up and follow. Roshan called out to it. The dog stooped and stretched on its forelegs, its hind wiggling, its mouth open in laughter. The woman smiled and the man touched his shoulder. Roshan called out to the dog, which came up to him and licked his hand. He stroked the white star on its forehead. 'Sirius,' the man said, naming the dog. The dog licked the man's hand. The dog trotted towards the shadows and stopped halfway waiting for Roshan. Roshan got up from his chair. The dog ran to him, took hold of his pyjama cuffs in his teeth and tugged at them. Roshan took his first steps into the emptiness, with Sirius by his side. The man and the woman followed, laughing. Their laughter was like flowers falling.

First, Roshan walked the emptiness gingerly and hesitantly, waiting for the hard things and the sharp angles to trip and hurt him. But Sirius was beside him, herding him with his nose and flanks, guiding his steps. Roshan quickened his walk, breaking into a hesitant trot. Then he began to run. He did not fall even once.

Reaching the other end of the emptiness, the living shadows enveloped him with low and cloying murmurs. In the forest, on the thick twisted vines, black roses grew. Moths with golden cuneiform on their wings lapped the dew. Roshan raised his hands and shouted in joy, laughing. Sirius barked and the woman laughed. Roshan hugged her tight, burying his head in the verdant thickness of her hair.

'Did your parents know?' Leena asks.

'They made a fuss,' the blind man says regretfully. 'Father shouted a lot and Mother cried. They took away the pup. It was smelling bad. The doctor came and bandaged my hands and applied stinging ointments to my face. It hurt.'

'Did you say they took away Sirius?' Leena interrupts.

'Not Sirius, silly, they took away the pup. Nobody takes away Sirius.'

He reaches out and scratches the air with long, restless fingers. Then he turns to her, sitting up in his couch.

'You shouldn't wear those glasses, Doctor, especially since you don't need them,' he says. 'They make you look too severe.'

'How do you know I am wearing glasses?'

'Sometimes we see what we are not aware we see.' He gets up. He whistles to his unseen dog and is gone.

Leena sits in the gathering dusk, the light of the table lamp getting brighter on the smooth-grained mahogany of the tabletop. The sleeves of her white cotton blouse are slightly wrinkled. She stretches out her long legs under her starched cotton sari. The wind is a cold murmur outside.

She smiles and takes off her glasses. She takes a little mirror out of her purse and applies red lipstick to her full mouth. She undoes her hairpins and her thick, curly hair falls around her shoulders.

'One does not always wish to see what one sees,' she says softly.

She picks up the file marked Roshan Sahai. It is becoming heavy.

* * *

SESSION THREE

Doctor's notes: *Paranormal fantasies with psychotic tendencies. To kill in order to possess. Signs of paranoia and psychopathic symptoms? But how did he know I wore glasses or that my lipstick was too pale? Wild guess, or did another sense become heightened to compensate for vision. Some kind of mental imaging faculty?*

'Tell me about Tina,' Leena says.

The blind man turns his face towards her. There is a small frown on his smooth forehead. Then his face clears.

'Oh, you have been reading the file on me that the Institution sent you.' He smiles. Then he throws his head back and rests it on his hands which are crossed behind the neck. He sighs.

'Ah, Tina!'

After the pup was taken away, Roshan's parents got him no more pets. But he didn't need any anymore; he had Sirius. The emptiness was not untraversable anymore and each time he wanted to visit the garden of the black roses, Sirius helped him to cross. He played among the thick trees and the dark grass, catching the iridescent moths in his palms. The moths slipped though his fingers in wisps of inky smoke, flitting about the black blooms in flashes of gold. Tired after play, he would lay his head on the lap of the woman who gave him the sleepy, sweet nectar of the sable flowers. The man too was there often, with his little wooden fiddle on which he played merry tunes, all the while taking dainty little steps on cloven feet. The music lifted the woman's hair like a living wind and the moths danced in its flow, among the roses. Sirius lay at the woman's feet, his tail wagging, tongue lolling, looking up at the fiddler and laughing.

But on lazy afternoons, while Mother slept her invisible sleep and Father was away, he would hear the voices of other children from the emptiness. It made him wistful and restless. They came from the void, but he longed to join them. Often, in the evenings, his parents would take him out when they went shopping and Mother would hold his hand so that he wouldn't fall. Roshan knew this was unnecessary since Sirius was always by his side. But that was his secret.

His parents took him to parks and sat him down on the grass. Father brought him cotton candy and ice cream. He sat licking the sweet, cold vanilla taste, his face turned in the direction in which the children played.

'Hey Rohit, I caught you!'

'Renuka, this isn't fair, I found it first ...'

'Vineet, Renu cheats!'

Roshan's mother sighed and rumpled his hair and drew him to her. He felt that her stomach had changed shape a little, it was definitely swollen. He placed a hand on her. He felt an undercurrent on the surface of his palm – a low, steady vibration.

'What has gotten inside you, Mother?' he asked.

Father laughed.

'We're getting you a playmate,' Father said. 'A little baby brother.'

'Or sister,' Mother said, with slight defiance.

His mother's belly swelled as the months passed, and the little drumbeat which came from within her sounded louder to Roshan's ears. He would spend hours beside his mother, face pressed to the taut dome of her stomach, feeling the growth of his playmate inside. Sirius lay beside him patiently, watching him with faithful eyes. The woman's visits had diminished, and often, when Roshan raised his steady gaze towards the garden across the void, he thought he glimpsed pale hair floating in the wind with black roses swimming in the tides. And Sirius would bark and wag his tail, looking at his master with expectant eyes. Sirius too had grown, his white coat thick and glossy, legs long and sleek. The white star on his forehead glowed in the void.

'My playmate is coming,' he whispered to Sirius. 'My baby brother. And she will come again to feed him black roses, just like she fed me.'

Sirius wagged his tail.

But when the child was born, the woman did not come. Mother placed the baby in Roshan's lap, and he felt its tender weight. Its presence called out to him from the void, making his chest hurt. He touched its stub nose and smooth cheeks, he took its little fist in his hand and felt his throat tighten.

'Your little sister, Tina,' Mother was crying. 'You are not alone in this world anymore.'

He learnt her with his touch and his lips, drinking in her baby odours, running his fingertips against the infant hardness of her gums, listening to the gurgle which rose in her throat, a cooing liquid gurgle, calling to the laughter which lay in his own. For Roshan was a boy who smiled a lot, as the neighbours said, but we've never heard him laugh, poor blind thing.

Roshan was always speaking to Tina, murmuring in a low, gentle voice to the little playmate who lay beside him in the void. He would feel her damp curls in his hand, sparse and soft, and run his palm along the soft contours of her face, trying to see it in his mind. He would speak to her about the fiddler in the garden, the golden moths that danced to his music, and the woman who was the mother of nectar. He told her about the Worldmakers and sang to her the lullaby of the dark garden's angels. Tina gurgled as if she understood, a beloved bloodsong from nowhere, and Roshan turned away to weep, burying his face in the thick hair of Sirius's coat. He felt a soft, familiar touch on the nape of his neck, the fragrance of green hair thick with roses. The cool dry lips brushed his ear.

'Don't cry, my dear,' the woman whispered, 'your little sister is here, with you.'

'She is not here,' Roshan answered bitterly, 'she is not real. She is just a touch, a voice, a smell. She is the ache in my breast that I cannot see.'

The void grew deeper and darker as if universes swirled within.

'You can make her real,' the woman said softly, her palm wet with his tears.

'You can make her real before the void takes her away.'

'Nothing can take her away,' Roshan said, clasping Tina to his chest. 'She is mine.'

He clutched her tight and the baby gasped. He held her even tighter and Tina began to cry.

'Hush!' he said, squeezing harder. 'No one will take you away from me.'

The baby was choking now, and he whispered to her not to be afraid, because Big Brother was with her, and he would set everything right and no one would take her away from him.

'Just let anyone try,' he crooned, squeezing her to him, and Sirius barked in agreement. He sunk his face in her flesh, inhaling deeply the odours of her skin, quieting her struggles. From the void, he heard his mother's scream, a long, high, animal wail of grief and terror. Her blow glanced off his back and he fell on his side, clutching Tina to him. The baby was quiet now, lying slack in his embrace, but he wouldn't let her go. Sirius was growling and he felt an excited babble of voices around, stinging him like wasps flying out of the void and the baby was wrenched away from his grasp.

Mother was still screaming. But the woman hushed him, surrounding him in the vast perfume of her green hair. She pointed out at the void. A little baby girl stood there, sucking on her thumb. Her skin was golden, her eyes dark roses, her hair soft and curly. She smiled at him shyly. Sirius ran to her, barking and wagging his tail.

'Tina, my little one,' he called out to her, getting up and then someone hit him a huge blow on the back of his head. The void closed around him.

In the doctor's consulting room, the sunlight is a butterfly, coming through the gauze curtains. It is a cold light, and it lies on the man's still face like winter on alabaster. Leena gets up to close the thick, green window curtains and turns on the lamp.

'You were taken away to an institution,' she says. 'But you were shifted every few years.'

'I wasn't lonely, I had Sirius and Tina,' the man says. 'But then there was this little pup in the place I was first sent to. Sirius too needed company. I knew he had no other dogs to play with.'

'And the little boy in the dormitory?'

'Oh, Raju? Why?' A sly look comes into his face. 'What about him? Why don't you ask Tina? In fact, it was she who wanted me to bring Raju to her.'

Leena shivers and looks towards the blind man on the couch.

'So, did you fill the void?' she asks.

The blind man's face is suddenly expressionless.

'Why do you ask?'

'Are Raju and Tina also with you here?'

'What do you know about them, Doctor?'

'You were telling me about the void …'

'It is no longer empty. The woman still lives in the garden across. We visit her, to pluck the black roses from her hair and listen to the music. But one day, Raju did not come back …'

'Where did he go?'

'I don't know. Maybe he got lost in the garden, maybe he went away with the man to learn the fiddle. When I asked the woman, she only smiled and shook her head.'

'Did Tina cry?'

'I haven't seen Tina either since yesterday.' His voice is high with hysteria. 'She said she was going to look for Raju. And she hasn't returned.'

Leena goes across to the man and touches him briefly before returning to her chair. Her touch is soft and cool.

'It is going to be just as it was in the beginning, isn't it, Doctor? Just the void and me,' he says. 'That's why I keep Sirius on a leash, so that he too doesn't leave.'

'Are you so afraid of the void, Roshan?' Leena asks him gently.

His laugh is harsh and flat.

'You are the doctor, you should know,' he says. 'You are the one who has been reading up on me in the files.'

Leena gets up and walks over to the blind man, pausing to pick up the hospital files from her table. She thrusts them into his hands, and his fingers feel them automatically. With a cry he lets them fall to the floor.

'Braille! Braille is what they taught me at the Institution!' he says. 'But how come you read …'

He stops and looks across in her direction, but Leena is too quick for him.

She leans over and quickly pushes his hands down and clamps the handcuffs over his wrists. Then she sits back and straps his legs to the couch.

'I have been waiting for you, Roshan,' she whispers in his ear, tasting the musky pollen smell of his earlobe. 'My void is utterly empty.'

He laughs, a mirthless flat noise.

'You aren't wearing your glasses, Doctor,' he says.

'I'm not wearing anything,' Leena murmurs, sliding over him, slipping her arms around him. She brings her mouth down on his, capturing his tongue and sucking on it. He cannot breathe. Somewhere at the back of her neck, the first small muscle of her embrace begins to tighten.

BIRJU

Manju Kak

Cupping my hands to my mouth, I giggled. I thought he looked funny. Startling glassy blue eyes, looking down his nose grandly. 'To be or not to be ...' he recited gravely. My giggles bubbled through again as my gangly legs dribbled a beat against the wall of the pigeon coop upon which I was perched; limp brown hair, Hitlerish moustache ... a Hamlet ... Why! He couldn't cut a tragic figure, ever! But Birju did so love to act larger-than-life roles, and I to watch. He was fanciful too and told tales. Yes, those are some of the things I remember even now, when I think of him sometimes, and wonder where he is.

Birju Mamaji was one of Nani's nephews. Though she was long dead, he continued to spend three long months with Nana every winter. It was the best season in the Gangetic plains. Nana sent a distant cousin, Iqbal bhai, to fetch me for the holidays and we arrived at Colonelpura after a few hours of rattling in a rusting, weather-beaten UP Roadways bus. In the monsoons, it was different, for the Ghagra river was flooded and in full spate. The busload got off at the ghat and woe if the steamer ferry had just left. It was then an easy two hours' wait for its return, carrying passengers who had embarked on the other side of the bank. This made the eighty-mile journey to Colonelpura from Lucknow interminably long, so then the driver would brook no conversation, no wayside stops for tea, pumping the accelerator desperately till the muddy monsoon waters of the river had been sighted with drooping figures waiting at the worn-washed, creaking, wooden ramp serving as its quay.

Iqbal bhai usually insisted on the bus but I preferred the train, though there was no direct one. It was an express pulled by a smoke-spouting steam engine that stopped at Bankipur junction, where painfully thin urchins did superb acrobatic contortions with their bodies, sending prickles down my spine. Like my fellow passengers, I would force my hand through the iron window bars to toss a few coins. They troubled me, those hungry faces, spoiling my magical reverie of homecoming. I wished they would go away, so that I could pretend that they didn't exist. I would wonder what kind of a life it was for beggars, imprisoned by the hope that coin-tossing passengers brought. My life was too distant for this contemplation. What need had I, going to Nana's in the starched crisp uniform of an English missionary school, to know of theirs? And by the time we changed platforms to catch the slow Colonelpura Passenger, I forgot them. The train chugged along another four stops, in pace with the stillness of life in our backwater town in the Gangetic plain. While I could sometimes persuade Iqbal bhai to take the train during the monsoons, in winter it was invariably the bus.

The winter I turned thirteen, Uncle Mannu was awaiting the arrival of the bus in his spanking new Fiat, dominating the bus terminus with his camaraderie, exchanging news with cronies and friends, being offered cups of tea and *paan*, cursing diabolical politicians with gusty fervour. Then, discovering the bus had arrived and was unloading, he rushed hurriedly in our direction to collect us, bag and baggage, hustled us into the car, and zoomed down an overcrowded bazaar road in a tearing hurry, avoiding near collisions with stray dogs, cattle, children, and little tin-sheeted stalls on shaky wooden stilts, incessantly blowing the horn. Street urchins chased the car gleefully and he too, childlike, enjoyed outracing them, till he would suddenly remember that he needed to stop for a minute. He always had to stop for a minute, diverse plans and errands preying on his mind as he drove; cigarettes from the *paanwala*, a message for the plumber via the cycle-*repairwallah's*, a reminder about a party at the District Club to Colonelpura's sole *khansama* who could do a soup and trifle. Then, as if it had just popped into his head he remarked: 'Birju's here.'

'Birju?'

I was surprised, excited and yet nervous. I looked forward to Birju's visits, not only because he had so many wonderful tales to tell but more because he shared and understood my fears of doing things that to others seemed so simple. Maybe he had them too, the fears. Of course, all through growing up, I knew Birju was different, but it was only on his last visit that I had realised why. I hesitantly asked Uncle,'Same?'

'Same,' he sighed, keeping his eyes fixed on the road.

I thought of that last day just before I had left. It was February 1960. Hearing a radio broadcast, Birju had gone rushing to the railway station to snatch an early morning paper. All the way back in a rickshaw, he either held his head in his hands or flung his arms out in the manner of an overblown stately tragedy, ranting at amazed passers-by, who gaped at his distress that the English Princess, Margaret, had chosen to marry a society photographer, a nobody – Armstrong-Jones.

'Come on,' I told Birju giggling, thinking he had fallen into another of his *roles*. But there was no mirth in his eyes, only the real pain of rejection and from within, a deep crying sorrow that laced his voice. My laughter dried up on me as I stared at him, confused. 'She promised she would wait for me,' he wailed. 'Women, fickle women, do they ever deserve good men?' He mourned the rest of the day, a symbolic black ribbon tied on his arm, adding to his sartorial elegance.

Of Birju, I must say, he was the best dresser I had seen then. Impeccably cut trousers and coats, and shoes that never looked as if they needed polishing. Moreover, he had no body odour, he never seemed to perspire like we did. In winter, he wore a stylish greatcoat that he had wheedled out of Nana, one that Nana had had stitched at Saville Row, on his only trip to London.

It was a game they played every time Birju visited. He would rustle through Nana's great wardrobe – warm glowing Burma teak, fronted by an elegant oval Belgian mirror. There would be bow ties, silk kerchiefs, shirts, and *achkans* stitched at the legendary Mohammadally's in Calcutta, and at the bottom, in neat rows, two dozen pairs of shoes. Apparel that Nana had given up wearing when he joined the Freedom Struggle, and had donned *khadi*. Also, they now sagged from his shoulders. But still he was loath to part with them, and never to his sons, whom he secretly considered sloppy. When Birju rustled through, Nana would make a great pretence of resistance, till Birju emerged in one of those excellent pieces, his hair slicked back, half-shut eyes glancing down his nose arrogantly, looking like a Hollywood hero of the forties. Yes, they were definitely meant for him. And Nana would sigh, silently regretting that none of his progeny had the carriage or the aquiline nose that lent Birju such distinction.

And that's how Birju had got the greatcoat.

When he wasn't there, I felt lost, missing the Birju who wove fantastic tales of places he had never visited – Madame Tussaud's, Hyde Park, Westminster Abbey, the Tower of London ... but which he described in such detail that I grew up believing he had actually been there. Oh yes, Birju's visits always brought fun. For otherwise, without him, Nana's house was as always. Nothing ever changed. A chipped piece lay unobtrusively, lovingly neglected till it became an accepted part of everything else. If removed, we'd have felt its absence as acutely as if it were an active part of our lives.

When bored, I usually went over the house carefully, furrowing into bookshelves filled with books turning sepia, in a large carved rosewood crockery cupboard, ending up at the steel Godrej almirah in which Nani's things were stored: silverware, sarees – grotesquely and richly embroidered (too expensive to throw and too old-fashioned to wear), her false teeth in a silver soap case, a lock of Mannu Uncle's baby hair. Mementos were undisturbed by spring cleaning or packing cases at Nana's.

But there was little time for pottering around when Birju was around. He would have read some more books the previous year and would narrate them, his eyes and brows moving like a Bharatnatyam dancer's, bringing a florid vivacity to the lives of King Lear, Mary Queen of Scots, Julius Caesar. He would enact with dramatic flourish the chivalry of Sir Walter Raleigh and the dastardly death of Beckett, all of which I enjoyed much more than Senior *Mamaji's* sonorous recital of the epic *Ramayana* with its predictable heroics and its inevitable triumph of good over evil. It didn't matter what we did together, doing water colours or clay toy-making, Birju always helped me to do it differently. Besides, unlike other adults, he never said I tired him out with questions. Rather, it was Uncle Mannu who tired him out. I thought Uncle Mannu resented Birju's privileged missionary school education that allowed him to speak English fluently. And Birju secretly despised Uncle Mannu for being a trifle boorish perhaps – umpteen curses delivered in a loud baritone, endless off-key singing, *paan*-spitting, his penchant for witless jokes, and so on. Sometimes, in his removed refinement, in his detachment from things real that plagued adults, Birju appeared almost spiritual, like a Jesus or a Moses in a Cecil de Mille biblical movie.

Now when I think about it, what did Birju not have! Looks, intelligence, lineage (maybe he had too much, which is why he seemed not to care for any of it). Only this one thing jarred. Nothing noticeable though. If you didn't know, you couldn't tell, and families hid their own frailties admirably then. Oh, he was alright really; he talked and laughed and argued intelligently on almost any subject. But that last visit, I had wondered if he was, whether he might be … no, no, no one said it openly ever … so when I asked Uncle – 'the same?', I supposed he knew what I was implying. All the way, sitting next to Iqbal bhai in the car, I worried about how I should greet him so he would not guess about my, at last, understanding *why* he was different.

Birju was sitting in the veranda facing the wide porch, in one of those great big basket chairs, watching the road languidly through half-shut eyes when we drove up. A curl of excitement wriggled within me. Momentarily forgetting my anxiety, I quickly jumped out of the car, telling him how happy I was to see him and asking – where had he been this time, what new books had he read and what-all had he done. But as I prattled on breathlessly, I knew it was coming out all wrong, for he responded with a distant cordiality he had never shown me before. Was it because I was now more grown up and the same familiarities would not do between a bachelor and a young woman? But for me, Birju had never been a man … sexless really.

That winter, Birju was more than frequently seen at Nana's neighbour's, the Principal Sahib, with whom he had long discourses on esoteric subjects and weighty tomes which I now doubted he had ever read. Though I worried about and mused over that shaded look in his eye that kept me at a small distance, the more I tried to bridge it, the more it yawned me away. He continued to avoid me that winter. It was easy in that large house. There was nothing I could do to un-know what I now knew, to draw him back into the warmth of companionship that my childhood innocence had allowed me to share. How could I know that it was just that which had hurt him, the shadow that had glazed my face, which had taken away from him a sense that he was an equal.

I hated it, this growing adulthood, that forced me to face reality at every turn, for Birju's world was of the unreal, and he had no room for those that lived outside it, or who chose to doubt his world's existence. Why had I begun walking out of it?

With the adults, it was different. He was in control. They laughed at him as he wanted them to, treating him like a joke, getting into heated arguments just to see him display his histrionics and crazy antics as they would watch a clown in a circus. He accepted it as his role, as a clown would his nose on stage, a part he played ... and would have been affronted if someone in the audience had shouted – Take it off, I know that's not really yours. Those were the rules of audience. But I didn't know that then.

Then came that early morning at the end of my holidays. Uncle's cousin, Markandey, came rushing with the news that Birju was seen at the station, trying to buy a ticket to Delhi against a newspaper clipping. Naturally, the ticketing clerk would not agree that it was legal tender. Birju had whipped up an aristocratic fury at which the Station Master had been summoned. Birju told him that there were things of national import taking place in Parliament and his advice was needed. It was imperative that irrelevant details like money be disregarded when a man of his calibre was required to set the Cabinet right. Swirling out his trump card, he talked of Prime Minister Nehru's daughter, Mrs Gandhi; she was his cousin, he said (and engaged to marry him once, except that he had objected to a blood match); anyway, she would hear of this impertinence – his not being allowed onto a filthy train, and he flapped himself into further fury. The last scenario, Markandey explained animatedly, was the Station Master on his knees, beseeching mercy, and Birju magnanimously unsheathing an imaginary sword and anointing him Knight of the British Empire. He had forgotten his Nehru-Gandhi connections and had become George VI.

Uncle's new Fiat was revved up and he drove post-haste, with Markandey hopping in, really to see the fun. A hot cup of station tea was needed to revive him, Uncle explained. But Uncle Mannu was raving angry. Being tolerated humorously by all who visited Nana's house was alright in its place, but humiliating the Station Master on his very own platform, with the coolies and passengers looking on, was going too far.

Uncle, who was Birju's age, gave him a dressing-down right there on the platform, allowing the Station Master to retrieve some of his lost dignity. 'That madcap ought to know better,' he shouted to his audience, as he commandeered his cousin into the car. Birju clambered in meekly, slamming the door behind him, pulling the windows up, foetus in a womb.

Uncle continued to fume on the platform: this was carrying pretence too, too far, he continued. Pretence, the Station Master asked? Pretence, he stamped; he was sure all this madness was humbug, a guise for not taking a job. But those trips to the – the Station Master interrupted. Pchah, spat Uncle, all for a free life, wanting everything free, he scoffed. That Birju was always a bounder. Ran through his father's fortune, dropped out of college ... now all he can be is mad, convenient, huh! Or a clerk, much harder work that, he sniggered, and not quite in keeping with his English education. A clerk! And he guffawed aloud. A nobody, he would be then huh? Didn't want to be a nobody, did he? But mad ... that makes him *somebody* ... and he burst out laughing again.

When the car pulled up, Birju dismounted, beaten and sad, his greatcoat sagging at his shoulders. While Nana and Senior

Uncle noticed his drawn looks that evening, there was nothing that could be said or done. For Uncle Mannu would not apologise. What for? he asked. For merely telling the truth?

I was confused. This world of grown-ups was hateful, I thought, for if Birju wished to be mad, why didn't Uncle let him be so?

Birju was unusually quiet at dinner. He had shed all his roles. The next morning, he came around to the front veranda holding his brown leather bag. Everyone was seated with newspapers and tea. 'Send for a rickshaw, I'm going to the station,' he announced, not looking anyone in the eye. Nana gently tried to dissuade him. 'It's over, Birju, we all lose our tempers.' But, taciturn yet dignified, Birju repeated his request firmly.

That morning, Birju left. He never came back. I turned fourteen and fifteen and sixteen. Sometimes Senior Uncle would wonder aloud about him, and so would the rest of us. Uncle Mannu would snigger – sponging off some other relative, I suppose. Tales sometimes filtered in from Lucknow – he was seen lunching at the Carlton. From Kanpur or Hardoi – Birju was seen walking past the flats in Naini Tal. Or the Mall in Shimla. So the bugger's cooling off in summer, Uncle smirked. Which sucker has he caught this time? Slowly, no news came any longer. In time, I forgot about him.

It must have been two decades later. Dragging along two whining kids, I was shopping in Lucknow's crowded Hazratganj. I came down the wide stairs of Mayfair, to the chaotic main road lined with balloon sellers, hairclip vendors, and hawkers of sundry things. Tripping clumsily, I fell, scattering the shopping bags I was carrying.

Someone stooped to help. Turning, I saw him. I jerked away; one never knew what diseases they carried, these beggars. Then, ashamed, I stretched out guiltily to put a coin in his hand, moving on to hail a rickshaw. That greatcoat? I swiftly turned around and saw him looking at me. Birju? There, squatting on the pavement, in Nana's coat! Hot flushes rose in a volley ... and then I wanted to run and retrieve the coin ... to ask him where he had been all these years ... to ask him why he had never returned ... to take him home. Yet, I hesitated. He saw it in my eyes as he had done once before, and in his own blue ones came the same knowing look that he had had that winter. He immediately looked away as I did too, pretending it was all a mistake. Rattling his beggar's bowl, he began to sing discordantly. Quicker than I, he had put on his clown's nose – for me, adult now – and I couldn't shout to him to take it off. The rules of audience prevailed. What's happened Mum, who is it? the kids tugged. They prodded on as children do. I heard myself replying, as if from afar – no one, no one really ... just someone I thought I once knew and, shame shadowing me, I crossed the road.

THE DAY OF THE FUNERAL

Binoo K. John

Actually it wasn't the end, after all. After her man had died the previous day, bringing to an end about four decades (she was not quite sure when they had got married) of living together in silence, Grandmother felt a strange confidence about the future. But on the day of the funeral, she could not believe that Grandfather was actually gone.

She found herself thinking of the faraway days when hope used to rise in her with every breath she took. In the innocence of her virginal adolescence, when she had walked behind Grandfather on the day of her marriage to the wood-carved manor, and she had asked him,

'Why are you not saying anything to me? I can understand and speak your language.'

Such innocent, and in retrospect, funny questions of doubt and frustration were to continue all her life, but it was almost always the other-worldly silence and a meaningless gaze, or at best, mumbled half-answers that she got from Grandfather. So if the truth had to be told, she would not miss her man. But yet, on the day of the funeral, she found tears cascading down her eyes, and dripping on to her white *mundu* till it became embarrassingly damp. She was sitting far away at the other end of the veranda of the huge big house where she had lived so long with her man.

She could not yet gather enough strength to go near her man and gape at his face once again, to see him lying there as if alive. She felt an urge to run her fingers along the contours of that face, something she had never been able to do during their living days. There were many others there in the house, pottering around, getting set to bury Grandfather, and all she was expected to do was to sit there and shed her forty years of tears.

Through her tear-filled eyes she looked back once again at her life full of questions and frequent outbursts of volcanic temper that had dissipated in the vacuum of silence that enveloped the manor. Caught in the cocoon of silence, she too had forgotten to converse with Grandfather who always talked in half-finished sentences that had a ring of finality to them.

Yesterday, on the eve of his death, when the clouds had gathered and the winds blowing in from the Kodoor river sounded like a dirge, Grandfather had looked into her eyes and spoken:

'I am going. You will have to be alone now.'

For one searing moment of anger and apprehension, she thought her man was mocking her, with a departing bout of sarcasm.

Gopalan, the labourer, was there too, and so was the village baker Avaran, who had come with some freshly baked bread and little, rounded sponge cakes that were his speciality. Grandfather spoke to all of them in incomplete sentences that most of them nevertheless understood.

Through the prism of tears in her eyes, the cameos from the past suddenly flashed before her. Yesterday, when Grandfather had called her and looked into her eyes and told her of his impending death, there had actually been a nerve-tingling sense of longing and romance which he had never really shown all the years they had lived together. Some of the women who used to come to work there during the harvest had told Grandmother that her man really adored her; why else would he always be looking towards the kitchen?

That day, when he told her that she would be alone now, not sadness, but anger swelled in her and the words came gurgling up from within her,

'The moment you go, I will be free of solitude.'

The words almost never came out when she saw death in his eyes.

She knew quite well how to read his eyes and the changing contours of his silent face. Grandmother always felt that he actually wanted to talk to her, in long drooling sentences, weighed with meaning if not much clarity, but actually never really managed to.

When he said those parting words, she knew he was talking of a love that bound them together in silence and solitude. Hearing of that love, she held the corner of the towel that always hung on her burdened shoulders and wiped the tears that escaped spontaneously from her eyes.

Avaran pretended not to have seen this and started counting the sponge cakes, pushing them towards the old couple who had discovered love on the threshold of death.

'Mother, here are the cakes. Give it to Grandfather also.'

She was the mother to all the outcasts who served the landed gentry. Those rare souls, who came at different times of the day and stood near the veranda, not venturing to climb up and sit there; these were her links with sanity and the outside world.

Yesterday, both Gopalan and Avaran had seen death in Grandfather's eyes and both had moved out, leaving the old couple to live out their last flickering moments of love together. Even in that moment, when they should have talked of the love that bound them together in their silence, she could not say anything. She felt so defeated.

The tears were all she had to show for Grandfather. They were the tears of her life that came gushing, washing off all her years of anger and frustration. After a long time, who knows how many years, of silent togetherness, her uncontrolled sobs spread through the dark wide expanse of the village manor.

As a teacher of Shakespeare, he was a different man altogether. When, for instance, he taught the storm scene in King Lear, words poured out of him and transported the students to another age and time. But outside the classroom, his powers of persuasion often failed him, and the flood of words was locked in by some guttural sluice-gate. Once he reached his house on the banks of the Kodoor river, he receded into silence and his trademark half-finished sentences.

The day he came back from school for the last time after serving for thirty-five years (barring the last six months when schools were closed due to a students' strike demanding equal fees for private and government schools), everyone who came to meet him believed that this great English teacher would not last long without being able to talk to students about Shakespeare. But he surprised everyone in the village and lived on for five more years.

Grandmother too thought of the day he had retired which, like the day of his death, was an important benchmark for her to look back into the vacuum of silence which she inhabited. During many such days of peace (and needless to say, silence) when everything was calm, unlike on the day of the funeral when there was an upheaval of sadness, Grandfather's wife would appear on the veranda and lean on a mahogany pillar, one of the five that rose up from the veranda to support the slanting roof. She never gave up hope that they could talk like long-lost friends.

Grandfather sat for long hours at the other end of the veranda on his long-armed planter's chair with *The Complete*

Works of Shakespeare within hand's reach on the ledge of the wooden wall carved out of teak. It was near where the Bible was kept. It was only when the postman came with the pension that he ventured to get up or when someone asked him to take a look at the harvesting of grain.

Avaran or Paravan Thampi, the coconut plucker who climbed palm trees with the swiftness and ease of a monkey, or a labourer on his way from the fields, would sit there talking to him on many days. They sometimes managed to get Grandfather to say something substantial. But apart from the rare occasion, no such voice came and they all knew he resided in another world and respected him for it.

'Thampi, tomorrow we will need ten tender coconuts. The children from Kadamaserry are coming,' Grandmother would join in the conversation.

On other days, when there were no relatives or children expected, Grandmother, living out the haunting loneliness of her life, would find out about the outside world, the prices of things in the market, or the upcoming festival in St. George's Church by talking to the labourers who came there.

'How far has the road reached, Gopala? Are they not digging day and night?'

'Coconuts should fetch more than one anna for a dozen.'

'Yohannan, why don't you plant tapioca in that grove? Make some money for yourself.'

This was how Grandmother communed with the world. When there was a marriage or a baptism in her ancestral house across the river, Grandmother would start thinking of it many days ahead of the event. She would even send Gopalan in the boat to Kollamthara to inform her folks about her impending visit. Actually her mind never left her own family house, which was always boisterous with joy and cluttered with unannounced guests, and unending food that spread the aroma of content.

Through all such snatches of conversation, Grandfather sat detached on his cane-woven planter's chair, his legs resting on the long arms.

For brief moments when he came back to earth, he looked straight ahead at the wooden gate with spikes and asked:

'How was the harvest?'

Often his wife answered the question in the hope that it would spark off a conversation with her husband and convince her that his lifelong silence was just a momentary aberration.

'Better than last time,' she would say, glancing from behind the mahogany pillar at her husband, hoping like she did every time that his eyes would meet hers.

They seldom did for the forty years or so that they lived in the manor, but she somehow convinced herself that in the anonymity of the night's darkness, when even the ripple of the river's little waves pushing against the mud banks of Kodoor could be heard, his eyes looked into hers.

But with the light of day, he assumed a strange silence and detachment as he slipped into the rarefied world of Shakespeare that he spent his day in. The same Shakespeare – King Lear and the other tragedies that he tried to get the school students interested in. For all that lifelong effort, he was often derided by students who sometimes hid behind coconut palms and shouted 'Hello, King Lear', as he walked to and from school.

Now all that was over. And all that was left for Grandmother to do was to walk aided by one of the women there, and go and plant that last kiss on his sunken cold cheeks, and leave behind a smudge of her wet tears on his face.

After that, Grandmother would be free.

THE LADIES' GHAT

Pavan K. Varma

Ghazipur was distinguished for being so completely like what every small district town in eastern Uttar Pradesh is: small, dusty, poor, dirty, and full of the largely futile cacophony of *mofussil* India. But there was no break of any length from school that did not see me there, within the walls of my ancestral home, Pulkavali. Pulkavali was built by my grandfather. It was the only home he knew, and he had built it lovingly from the money earned fighting the cases of the numberless litigants swarming around like ants, forever in search of an anthill they could call their own.

My grandmother was beautiful, but docile, reconciled to the inequity of a world ruled by men. She came from a very well-known family in nearby Benares, but her husband was merely an impoverished lawyer when she married him. They were married when they were both not more than fifteen. It is said that on his first day of court, he came to his wife and asked her to give him her gold bangles. She did so immediately, and without asking why. He pawned the bangles, and got himself a buggy to ride to the *kutcherrie*. He could not, he said, go to court, even on the first day, without the trappings of a style which he felt was his due. He was an imperious man, a great disciplinarian, who gave a lot of importance to notions of family prestige and respectability.

His arrogance of spirit held him in good stead, not least because it was accompanied by a great deal of talent and hard work. In but a few years, he became the leading lawyer of Ghazipur. And Pulkavali was built and grew and flourished along with his success.

There was one thing above anything else that redeemed Ghazipur for me as a child. And that was the river Ganga. Pulkavali was built close to its banks and much of my vacation was spent on the ghats, visible in the distance from the gates of the house. One holiday, when I was thirteen, is particularly well etched in my memory.

To witness the sunrise from the ghat will always remain one of the benedictions of my childhood. Of course, there was activity on the ghat even before the sun came up. Some devotees came for their prayers and ablutions when the night was about to end, and the dawn was still a promise. The sun rose fragile, like porcelain in gold, held up precariously against the still darkened sky almost against its will, and I often thought that it was about to give up its burden and slip silently into the deep ochre waters of the river. But the miracle of a new day prevailed. There was the sound of temple bells, and in the cool morning breeze, the sound of the sacred chants.

The men used one section of the ghat, the women another. As a child, I used to be fascinated by the ability of the women to bathe in the river with their saris on, without exposing their bodies, although the older women were less careful, or perhaps less concerned about what people saw. I was particularly taken up by how the women would change out of their wet saris and blouses into the clothes they had brought

En route to the Landour cemetery with Ruskin Bond.
Left to right: Meenakshi Kumar, Aditi Khanna, Ruskin Bond, Pooja Jain, Madhu Tandan, Shiela Reddy, Anita Joshua, Bulbul Sharma, and Nemita Gokhale.

The tombstones have many a tale to tell: Ruskin relates the stories of British officers whose graves lie sheltered among the deodars.

While Ruskin held the attention of the group with yet another story of the graves, his own face and fame as a storyteller, brought the cemetery chowkidar's little son running to ask him for an autograph.

The hub of Landour, Char Dukan, *with the proverbial seat around the central tree, which has, no doubt, witnessed the exchange of confidences, arguments, and philosophies. Seated from left to right: Ganesh Saili, Rupin Desai, Renu Varma, and Mimi Kapoor.*

Manju Kak and Shiela Reddy enjoy a relaxed, comfortable camaraderie amidst sessions at the Retreat with others.

Madhu Tandan, taking a break from dream analysis, while Namita urges eager questioners to join them for a walk.

with them. My vantage point was a stone platform under a large mango tree overlooking the bathing area. From this perch, I could see very clearly how they went about this difficult task. First, the wet sari and petticoat had to be jettisoned, but without anything showing. The technique lay in deftly slipping over the head the petticoat waiting to be worn, and then with that as a covering, quickly unwinding the sari and opening the wet petticoat and wriggling out of both. But the more difficult task was wearing the blouse. This required great coordination. The older women did it with practised ease. The younger ones often had to struggle. While the dry petticoat was propped over the body by the use of the elbows, and with one corner held by the teeth, the hands were manipulated into the blouse. But often, for one split moment, the breasts would be exposed as the petticoat was finally released to slip down to the waist. With the blouse and petticoat in place, the rest was easier: the blouse was hooked in place at the back, and the sari quickly worn over the whole. Some women left immediately after this. Others, usually the younger ones, combed their hair, and with the help of a small mirror, applied kohl to their eyes, put on a *bindi*, and, if married, added *sindoor* to the parting of their hair.

I found that sitting on my perch under the mango tree, overlooking the ladies' bathing ghat, was becoming part of my morning routine. There was no conscious planning in this. I would go to the ghat every morning, but after a dip and perhaps a *dona* of hot *jalebis*, my feet would, almost against my will, take me to that spot under the mango tree. Here I could watch, safe from discovery, unless one of the ladies deliberately looked up to see if anyone was peeping down at them.

I first saw her walking with a group of older ladies towards the ghat. I had never seen a more beautiful woman. She was not very tall, but her face, outlined by the *pallu* of her sari covering her head, was mesmerising. There was *sindoor* in the parting of her hair, and her hair, untied, could be seen extending to her waist. Although obviously newly married, she had an unselfconsciousness about her that was very sensual. All the ladies seemed to be laughing about something she was saying, and she herself joined in the laughter, throwing her head back, her nose pin catching the sun, her pearl white teeth glistening.

I watched her approach the ghat with a quickening of my heartbeat I had not known before. She stood at the edge of the river, scooping the water in her palm. Then she lifted her sari upto her knees and ventured into the water. I could hardly breathe. But then she abruptly stepped back. I could hear snatches of conversation. The older women were telling her to bathe, but she was saying the water was too cold, and that today she would only wash her face, and seek the blessings of the river. The other women told her not to create a fuss. The water was warm enough, they said. She remained unconvinced, but finally promised to come again the next day and take the ritual dip.

I could feel an acute sense of disappointment, and it must have shown on my face when I returned home, for my grandmother asked if I was feeling well. I was distracted throughout the day. The vision of her walking to the ghat kept pounding inside my head. As evening approached I was overtaken by a feeling of feverish anticipation, riddled with uncertainty. What if it rained the next day? What if she never really meant to fulfil the promise she had made? At night, I slept fitfully, and my dreams had a strange intensity to them.

The next morning I left for the ghat much earlier than usual. There was hardly anyone there. My eyes were pinned on the pathway that ended in the steps leading to the ladies' ghat. It felt like each minute was an hour. Some women came, bathed and left. I hardly noticed their presence. It was getting late. The sun was rising in the sky. Soon it would be too late. Grandmother expected me to be home for breakfast by eight.

The start of the first session outside the picturesque home of the Kapoors in Landour. Pensive, smiling, dreamy, observant – the expressions vary as thought processes are set in motion. In front, from left to right: Priya Kapoor, Pramod Kapoor, Mini Kapoor; Seated at the back: Kiran Kapoor, Namita Gokhale.

Bulbul Sharma, Namita Gokhale, Shiela Reddy and others getting ready to watch a quick improvisation on Hamlet.

A tea break in the midst of an animated discussion on the potency of the print word vis-à-vis the electronic blitzkrieg. Left to right: Aditi Khanna, Namita Gokhale, Mini Kapoor, Keki Daruwalla, and Priya Kapoor.

I got up to return, when, almost like a miracle, I saw her coming down the pathway, alone.

This time there was no hesitation in her demeanour. She placed her change of clothes at the water's edge. Looking around to see if anyone was there, she dropped her *pallu*, tied her hair in a bun and waded into the water. When the water was waist deep, she stopped, closed her eyes, and took a full dip. For a moment she could not be seen, and then she emerged, her sari clinging to her body, her tresses dripping water. My heart was in my mouth. My palms were sweating. When she began to change, I thought she would be able to hear the beating of my heart. The dry petticoat came on as an awning. With a fluidity of movement I have never been able to forget, she was soon out of her wet sari. But as she struggled to wear her blouse, the petticoat fell, a little too early, to her feet. At that moment, the cosmos stopped. Involuntarily, she looked up. Her eyes met mine. And then I ran home as fast as I could.

I was out of breath when I reached home. My ears were burning. I felt a strange mix of both guilt and exhilaration. At breakfast, I almost died when Grandfather asked me why I took so long to come home. Rai Bahadur Loknath Prasad was coming home to introduce his newly wedded son and daughter-in-law, he said, and he wanted me to be around. The son had done very well, Grandfather said, as he sipped his bowl of milk. He was an engineer and had got a very good job in Calcutta. His wife came from a well-known family of Ranchi.

Neither Mr Prasad nor the achievements of his son interested me at that moment. My thoughts were elsewhere, but I did as I was told and quickly changed into a fresh *pyjama-kurta*. The Prasads arrived in a brand new Ambassador car. It was a gift from the girl's side, the Rai Bahadur said. The son wore a brand new suit, with very polished shoes. He shook my hand warmly, and asked what I wanted to be. An engineer like him? And then he beckoned to his newly wedded wife to meet me. She was talking to my grandmother, when she turned towards me. It was her.

My blood froze. My heart stopped. Grandfather was standing next to me, with that smile of pride and affection on his face. Suddenly a silence seemed to have overwhelmed the gathering. Everybody was waiting for the young bride to meet me. There was no question that she recognised me. For a moment she hesitated. My world was held in balance. And then with a faint smile on her lips, she walked up to me and took my hand in hers.

The next day she left with her husband for Calcutta. I never saw her again.

INCERTITUDE IS THE FORTRESS

R.W. Desai

Studying her face in the big bathroom mirror of the hostel, it suddenly struck Mona, a thirteen-year-old schoolgirl, that she bore a striking resemblance to her uncle, her *chacha*. Since she was very fond of him, this afforded her great satisfaction. She had been examining her pimples – youth blossoms – her mother had called them, but Mona hated this description, and barely refrained from squeezing and draining them of their contents, only because of her mother's warning that the scars would then persist all her life. The euphemistic term 'youth blossoms' bothered Mona. It was an abuse of language, she felt.

She had developed an unusual affection for words and liked to see them treated with respect. This had pleased her English teacher, but had also worried her a little because she felt that Mona might lose touch with reality in her obsession with words. Mona loved the sounds of certain words, their flavour, and the images they conjured up in her mind. To her, 'youth blossoms' was a horrible incongruity, a cruel misnomer. Everyone around her spoke of *youth* as a time of excitement, enterprise, and adventure, and *blossoms* was a word Mona had particularly relished for its sound, suggestive of *bloom* and *blown,* from which it was derived.

'Hating your features, or admiring them?' Sapna, her classmate, asked laughingly, as she came out of the shower in her dressing gown.

'No, hating my pimples,' Mona said bitterly.

'Oh, don't worry, they'll disappear as you grow up and acquire some sense,' Sapna said in a bantering tone.

Mona flung a handful of water at Sapna who squealed and vanished around the corner of the open door. Despite her disgust with her pimples, Mona liked the shape of her nose. It was a long, slightly curved, aristocratic nose that gave her face character and, being a tall girl for her age, and likely – everyone said – to still grow considerably, she was cultivating the fine art of looking down her nose with supercilious disdain at the lesser mortals who grovelled around her. Mona loved to render her thoughts and feelings into language, to savour the way in which the words she chose helped her understand herself better. She decided that *aquiline* was a good word to describe her nose, and she liked the sound of the word. Derived from aquila, the Latin for eagle, Mona felt that she deserved to move in such lofty circles.

Meanwhile, Sapna had come back, now dressed in a stylish housecoat and operating a portable hair dryer.

'Have you read the chapter on reproduction from *The Miracle of the Human Body* for Sister Emily's class?' Sapna asked.

'Yes, I read it last night.'

'Well, what do you make of it?'

Mona felt inferior to Sapna in this area. Though towering above her in height, and leaving her nowhere in basketball and hockey, Mona had to acknowledge that in human affairs, Sapna was worldly wise and knew her way around. Sapna had even boasted that she had two boy friends in Delhi who had written her love letters, but since she hadn't shared the letters with her friends, the claim was regarded as dubious. Accordingly, Mona was reluctant to confess to Sapna that the chapter had left her thoroughly confused, and that she hoped Sister Emily's class lecture would shed more light on the subject. It was evident to Mona that Sapna was eager to show off her knowledge, but at that moment, a noisy bunch of juniors invaded the shower area, and the conversation came to an end.

The study of Biology opened Mona's eyes to the mechanics of reproduction, an aspect of life that had hitherto been a closed book to her. True, not too long ago, when she was on the brink of puberty, her mother had prepared her for the changes she could expect within her body, and their disconcerting external manifestations, but had not gone beyond these. Hence the question of the male and female roles in the reproductive process, though animatedly discussed in the juvenile circle to which Mona belonged, yielded much interesting speculation but very little enlightenment.

It was in Sister Emily's class that enlightenment came. A kind old nun in a white hood – and nothing could better this Yeatsian description – Sister Emily introduced the class to its mysteries and gave the girls their first insight into the complicated role that they, as women to be, were destined by Nature to play, in being the creators, the bearers and the nurturers of new life. By contrast, Mona was shocked at the miniscule and ephemeral role that the male played in this strange encounter of the sexes. Obviously, there was no such thing as fatherhood, only motherhood. This conclusion she reached after discovering that even if the father was long since dead, the baby would still be born, in no way impaired by his disappearance.

'So the male has no importance after the act of fertilisation?' an incredulous Mona asked Sister Emily in class, when questions were invited at the end of the lesson.

Sister Emily smiled. 'Biologically, no,' she conceded. 'But in every other respect, yes.' Sister Emily explained that, by this, she meant that the father's role was supportive throughout the nine months of pregnancy, and thereafter. Mona was still not impressed. 'But that supportive role,' she argued, 'can be performed by anyone else as well – say the grandmother, or a sister, or even a good friend. There's nothing special about the father.'

Most of the other girls in the class were inclined to agree with Mona that Nature was being grossly unjust to the male of the species for having rendered him superfluous, but the others – and Sapna belonged to this group – felt that Nature had let off the males too lightly, that Nature had been unfair to the females for making them carry the entire burden of motherhood. At the same time, the whole class recognised the enormity of the responsibility and the power that they wielded as life's torch-bearers, a privilege denied to the males.

'Well,' Sister Emily concluded, after the bell rang, 'this is Nature's plan and we can't fight against it.'

That night, as Mona lay in bed on the point of falling asleep, and while her mind was still grappling with, and trying to assimilate, all that she had encountered in the classroom, her memory travelled back, quite unaccountably and quite suddenly, to a time when she was about six years old, as she now recalled. By now, she had shaken off her sleepiness, and felt quite startled by the clarity with which she could recollect what she had seen, its meaning unknown to her at that time.

She had woken up, she remembered, in the middle of the night on account of a bad dream and had screamed, 'Ma, ma,' and embarked on some kind of tantrum. Then her mother had appeared in the doorway of her bedroom in her nightie, her hair open and falling over her shoulders, had sat on the edge of her bed, soothed her, and patted her back to sleep. But Mona remembered that she had not really gone back to sleep, but lay in a kind of blissful, comatose state. A few minutes later her mother had withdrawn unobtrusively.

Quite inexplicably, Mona had then got up noiselessly and

peered over the top of the banisters down into the dimly lit drawing room. The table lamp shed a small circle of light on the carpet, and no other light was on. She could just see a part of the drawing room, including the huge maroon, plush sofa with its silver and gold embroidered cushions lying awry and, alongside them, two pairs of feet and, most curiously, one pair in the normal position in which feet are supposed to be – the position in which she had always seen her own two feet whenever she had looked at them while lying in her bed, the toes sticking up, pointing at the ceiling – but, quite unaccountably, there was another pair of big feet extending a little beyond the first pair and upside down, the toes pointing downwards.

Mona had soundlessly stolen a few steps down the staircase from where she had a better view of the sofa. Her mother lay on it on her back, her head resting on a cushion, her eyes closed, her hair spread untidily over the armrest of the sofa, and on top of her was her uncle, whom she recognised by his bald crown which was encircled by a fringe of thick curly black hair. He was evidently holding her down since there was some sort of a peculiar struggle going on. Mona remembered that she had wondered whether her mother was in some kind of difficulty, and whether she might need her help, but then she had heard her mother's soft, musical laugh, and she knew by that that all must be well. 'The games grown-ups play,' she had said to herself, 'and then they complain if I and the *dhobin's* daughter become a little rough when we play together.'

Mona's uncle, her father's brother, was a bachelor and a frequent visitor to the house. At that time, her father was away in Australia on a six-month government assignment to study the use of alcohol in automobile engines, and this naturally meant that her uncle would drop in frequently to find out if everything was all right, or if they needed his assistance. Mona was very fond of her uncle. He was very rich, had two big cars, a huge apartment, and was great fun. He was never tired of playing with her, and loaded her with presents.

By now Mona had lost interest in the scene in the drawing room since nothing seemed to be happening and, feeling sleepy, had crept back to bed and instantly fallen asleep. In the morning, when she awakened, her nocturnal experience had held no significance for her, but now, long after, as a consequence of Sister Emily's Biology class, that scene assumed a significance that greatly intrigued Mona. Were her mother and uncle doing together on the sofa what Sister Emily said all of Nature's creatures, including men and women, did? Of course, that was it, and she hadn't known a thing! It was an exciting thought. If only she had known, she wouldn't have crept back to bed. From the top of the stairs she had had a wonderful view, and she had stupidly gone back to bed!

Now Mona tossed and turned for a long time till, exhausted, she dropped off into fitful sleep. In the intervals, when she awoke, a nagging question that refused to go away was whether she was her father's niece, or her father's daughter. Like Alice in Wonderland in a different situation, Mona found the paradox disturbing, but also amusing. Might not the affair between her mother and uncle, which could have commenced much earlier, have resulted in her own conception? Might not the scene she had witnessed been a continuation of such scenes that had taken place times without number in the past? After all, her father, being a prominent scientist, often went abroad on important assignments.

Since she was still new to these momentous biological issues, she wondered whether marriage was an essential prelude to conception. She was almost sure that with human beings, such was indeed the case. At the age of thirteen, in a boarding school of Nainital where kind old nuns in white hoods abounded, the reality of unwed mothers was something unheard of. Mona hoped that her supposition was indeed the case, but deep down she had an uneasy feeling that that would be too good to be true. Marriage, after all, was but a man-made institution, and Nature had her own laws that man could only discover, not change.

At first, she considered asking Sister Emily, but then decided that Sapna might be a less intimidating source of information. If Sapna showed any uncertainty, she would then double-check with Sister Emily.

Sapna laughed loud and long when Mona put the question to her that evening. Sitting on her bed and brushing her bobbed hair, Sapna stopped the rhythmic motion of her arm and looked at Mona in utter disbelief. 'Of course, you silly thing,' she trilled, 'marriage has nothing to do with pregnancy, so you'd better be careful you remain a good girl till you're married, and after that you can do as you please. You have my full permission.'

Mona squirmed inwardly on hearing this light banter of Sapna's. Little did Sapna know that Mona's mother was quite possibly a living example of this advice, or that she herself was most probably the product of it. Outwardly Mona maintained an impassive expression. At thirteen, this may not be an easy thing to do, but Mona had acted in several school plays, and been complimented for her fine stage presence.

That night, when all the girls were in bed, Mona went to the bathroom – she could always claim she had a tummy upset if Sister Clara was on the prowl – switched on all the lights, and once again studied her face in the mirror carefully. It was unmistakable. She had her uncle's narrow, hooked nose, not her father's, which was broad and fleshy, and now, looking at herself critically and objectively, she could see that she was indeed a very good-looking girl – something she had never been really conscious of earlier, even though everyone had paid her this compliment as far back as she could remember – thanks to her uncle's role in her conception. For, by now, Mona was convinced that she was indeed her uncle's daughter. That she had inherited the shape of her face, a perfect oval, from her mother was, of course, not surprising. She remembered an old joke whose meaning she had never fully fathomed – Mama's baby, Papa's maybe – but which now was crystal clear to her, and she wondered how many of her ignorant classmates were in the same situation in which she found herself.

And now Mona wondered what she ought to be feeling – Outrage? Shock? Anguish? She examined her feelings, and saw quite clearly that she was feeling none of these. With her mastery over vocabulary, terms like *identity crisis*, *rejection syndrome* and *split personality* revolved round and round in her head, but she found them more interesting than disturbing. She debated within herself whether these were descriptions of actual mental states and situations, or whether they weren't lexical creations that had, through repeated usage, acquired a power of their own, independent of any reality. Did not these terms create reality, she wondered. For, as far as she was concerned, she did not feel any undue disturbance at the possibility of her uncle being her father, and her father, her uncle. *What difference does it make?* she asked herself. I'm still me.

Surprisingly, she could now look at herself from a detached standpoint, like a spectator watching a play, and tell herself how she ought to react. This capability gave her a wonderful feeling of release, as if she had freed herself from a bondage that was freighted with too much of the traditional, and was therefore not a help, but a hindrance. 'Obey your parents', 'Don't hurt their feelings', 'Don't let them down', 'Don't disappoint them', 'Fulfill their expectations' – these were barricades that had hedged her in hitherto; now she felt as if she could love both her father and her uncle in equal measure. Her uncle had risen in her emotional estimation, but her father had not gone down correspondingly, and Mona was glad that the status quo remained the same.

For if she was now convinced that she had her uncle's good looks, she was equally sure that she had been endowed with a goodly part of the intellectual baggage her father carried in his head. His influence had been, and still was, enormous. And, surprisingly, she had no ambivalent feelings towards her mother either. As far as Mona was concerned, she was a wonderful mother, and what right had she to point an accusing finger at her?

Mona did at one stage consider asking her mother about her paternity, but then decided against it. It was too risky. It would certainly affect her mother's attitude towards her forever afterwards. It would upset the family equilibrium. After all, what was the father's role in the whole business? According to Sister Emily, just a matter of a few seconds, and it was all over, though, as she had pointed out in considerable detail, his influence could be felt on an emotional and intellectual level after the baby was born, and this she had received in no small measure from her father. Biology was not everything, Mona decided. Certainty, after all, was but a fool's paradise. She switched off the bathroom lights and went back to the dormitory. Using her pocket flashlight she opened her locker and took out her Browning, her favourite poet. She turned the pages till she found *Rabbi Ben Ezra*, and read:

> Rather, I prize the doubt,
> Low kinds exist without,
> Finished and finite clods, untroubled by a spark.

Mona closed the book and went to bed, and to sleep.

RITES OF PASSAGE

Namita Gokhale

How does one write a made-to-order short story on themes of childhood, adolescence, and lost innocence? The questions perplexed me through many false starts, scratched-up beginnings, torn-up pages of ineffectual scribbling. To negotiate a short story successfully, one has to enter it gently and obliquely, glide on as effortlessly as possible, and then stop at precisely the mystic moment when the story must end. Timing is everything in a short story, and I find therefore that I am better at novels, where the reader is forced to be more tolerant of rambling.

It was on an airline flight that I finally got my opening. I was flying first class on a junket, and the air hostess was impossibly composed and elegant. She did not so much walk as glide, and I felt somewhat in awe of her incomparable elegance. I had a notebook balanced on my knees, and was as usual catching up with several conflicting deadlines. As she handed me a glass of champagne, I dropped my pen. Feeling impossibly clumsy, I bent down to pick it up. Suddenly I was on eye level with her perfectly shaped legs, and I noticed a large scar across her left knee.

Writers are fictionalisers by instinct, and I was immediately transported to a beautiful garden where this immaculate airhostess had once played as a child; I saw her running across this garden, which was a riot of joyous colours, and I saw her trip and fall over a bench and cut her knee. I could see the blood rushing out of the gash; I could almost feel her pain. It was all perhaps too terribly convenient in terms of my tearing deadline, for I had no proof or evidence that this was a childhood scar, but I chose to see it so.

All of us carry the visible and invisible scars of childhood within us. As we grow older, these become badges of honour and emblems of survival. I too have a gash on my left knee, and I can remember every detail of the hour and day I got it. My parents had left me in the care of my grandparents for a year and I felt both abandoned and indulged. I was thirteen, which is an in-between age betwixt and between the certainties of childhood and the bewilderments of adolescence. I too was running across a garden, not such a verdant and beautiful garden as I had imagined for the elegant air hostess, but a dusty New Delhi lawn, overrun with weeds, a humble lawn with many bald patches and overgrown untended flower beds, with phlox borders that crawled out of the coned brick boundaries into the exhausted lawn. There were four cane chairs in the centre of the lawn, and a cane table with a glass top. The cane chairs had recently been painted white, but I was not taken in by this cosmetic refurbishment. I preferred to sit on the scanty grass and have ants crawl up my legs rather than risk those vicious chairs. The chairs were full of splinters, and they practically leapt up to bite me every time I had made the mistake of trusting them.

I can still remember the book that I was reading that day. It was Albert Camus' *The Stranger* in a paperback English translation. I had received it as a birthday present on my thirteenth birthday from an intellectual cousin; not perhaps the most appropriate reading for an immature and bookish young girl, but it absorbed my attention and suddenly opened out a new and radically different way of observing life. I reread the passage where the hero looks at the night sky before he is about to be executed and understands the 'benign indifference of the universe.' I went back to the beginning and savoured the opening again. 'Mother died yesterday'… I read the sentence out aloud and felt very adult and grown up. It was growing dark in the lawn, and I had to strain my eyes to read, but I was reluctant to go back inside.

The telephone rang from deep within the house but I ignored it. My grandfather was not at home and neither was my grandmother. There were always servants around, or relatives; it was not the sort of household where the phone went unanswered. I shut out the shrill ring of the telephone, and continued to inhabit the new world and vision which the book had abruptly and unexpectedly opened up to me. But the phone continued to ring; I could not shut it out, and I ran across the lawn to get it. I was thin, knock-kneed and spindly-legged. With the characteristic clumsiness which I still spectacularly retain, I dashed across the lawn. The chairs did not get me, but the table did. I tripped and fell across the glass top of the cane table, and hot red blood gushed out of my knee. The cut was at least two inches across; it opened out like an evil mouth spouting out my lifeblood. I stared transfixed at the river of red which was pouring down my legs. It seemed unreal, ugly, and scary. I had never seen so much blood before.

I don't remember what happened after that – whether I cried out for help or if someone came out to help me. The old *pahari* servant, who ran the kitchen, poured sugar over the wound, explaining that this would help it to coagulate. Later, my grandmother bandaged it up, and I limped to bed feeling very sorry for myself.

I woke up before dawn to find a strange damp feeling

between my thighs. When I went to the bathroom to pee, I found that I was bleeding, not from my knee, which was still securely bandaged, but from somewhere higher up. I was perplexed and unprepared; nothing in my education or upbringing had prepared me for this.

That was the day I grew up. Like the beautiful airhostess, I carry the wound to this day.

THE RETIRED PANTHER

Keki N. Daruwalla

An hour after dusk, the panther would set out on his prowl, coming down the rain water ravine, skirting a patch of *ringal* reeds that he didn't like, past the forest fence, and then down the motor road going to Almora. Just below the road was a house built by a mountain lover from Faizabad, who came here for the summer. His wife had left a gap in the fence around their house where she had grown a lovely bed of narcissus. Through this gap, the panther would sometimes take his stroll and then go down the valley.

Time was, when he started from as far up as Saur Khal, the wild pig wallow, so named as it had been a place where boar were plentiful in days gone by. From Soowar to Saur was a phonetic transition that was easier on the tongue perhaps. (A sounder or two of wild pig were still around, but they were no longer the terrors they were once, despoilers of fields and disembowellers of men.) So far-ranging was the panther's beat when he was young, that he would go down the valley right till Bintha and Bhagwati Pokhar and those twin villages, Bunoli Malla and Bunoli Thalla. Those days, he went for boar and jackal, and only when he thought he was about to die of hunger would he attack a calf or goat kid. Now he was ageing, and the village drunk, on whom the Devi was said to descend during *ashtami*, had declared that the wretched fellow was gap toothed. Not that many would have volunteered to take a close look at his maw.

Subodh Singh was older than the panther. His knees were not what they used to be. In fact they were like the knees of some of the *chamchas* who surround our politicians. Subodh had other problems as well. The only son God had given him was a bit of an affliction. Subodh would blame it on sins he must have committed in some previous birth. These pre-natal, or earlier-incarnation sins give considerable solace to the peasantry in difficult days. Life would be unbearable without this unshakeable belief. If you haven't really sinned, or certainly no more than your neighbour, and still get your bones broken or your balls squeezed, how can you defend all this hocus-pocus about divine justice or karma? How handy the previous birth comes in here. It's a frigging godsend!

To revert to Subodh Singh's son, he could neither speak nor hear. He had named the child Ganga Singh, but Ganga soon turned into Gangua for his friends, and from Gangua to Goonga was but a natural step. The only thing the boy was capable of was minding cattle. But then Subodh didn't have many cows to boast of. It was as Shahji's cattleherd that Gangua made his living. He didn't have any friends either, except for Mansab Ali, the cook, who had come up with the Faizabadi couple. Mansab was as hard up for company as Ganga Singh. The mute boy was fun. Mansab found it exhilarating just trying to fathom what Gangua was attempting to say with a wave of his arm or a roll of his eyeballs.

Subodh did not allow his son to sleep alone. Suppose he

got a fit, or choked, or the panther came and knocked, as he often did? If there was a fire, he wouldn't be able to hear the crackle of dry grass and thatch. If there was an earthquake, how could he make out that eerie moan which comes wheezing and whining out of the very bowels of the earth? He wouldn't hear the dogs slavering at the mouth seconds before the tremors hit. The boy simply *had* to sleep in the same room as his parents.

There was one night when Gangua heard the panther's knock. The beast was known to have tried doors in the village earlier, especially of those rickety enclosures where cattle were tied. And of course there were occasions when he had succeeded in opening a door and getting away with a dog. Not many people were bothered. But if a calf was attacked, the entire village would raise a din and all hell would break loose. Gangua only noticed his presence that night because he felt the vibrations as the panther slammed his side against the door, and the house, half uneasy timber and half poorly mortared stone, shook like an autumn leaf in a gust of wind.

The day dawned clear and bright, two hundred miles of peaks covered with eternal snows looking down on the valley. A little cloud hovered, as always, over the flat razor-edged top of Nanda Devi. The villagers attributed this to the smoke from the cooking fires of Goddess Nanda. By noon, the cloud plumes had risen higher, but the *trishul* massif, with its three peaks, still towered over them. Nanda Ghunti, always overshadowed by Trishul, was veiled now. Nanda Kot, to the extreme right, looked the most photogenic – a white tent with a puff of cloud hovering over it like a benediction. But Gangua and his father were not exactly interested in the snows. They had gone around looking for pug marks first thing in the morning. When they saw the narcissus bed flattened, the one so carefully tended by the Faizabad couple, they were sure that the panther had come their way. The fellow must be really hungry, they rightly thought, for the full moon was just two nights away, and this panther had always shown a marked preference for shadows and the dark when it came to visiting the village.

A little scared with what had taken place during the night, Gangua kept his herd as near the town as possible. He was fond of his flock and he was very afraid of his mean old master, Shahji, who owned half the flats on the Mall and three or four grocery shops in the market. Life would be tough for his father if Shah threw him out of his job, something he often threatened to do. (Shah, of course, was never sure if Gangua had understood him right. Who can fathom the impact of words on the deaf?)

And then it happened. The worst thing about being prepared for the worst is that it happens. Gangua had taken no chances, keeping his dog in front and himself at the rear of the herd. Every now and then, he made odd clicking sounds, his tongue darting out like an ant-eater's. But it didn't keep the panther away. Those familiar with accounts of big game hunters will be disappointed that none of the usual warning signals were forthcoming. No *sambhar* belled, no *kakar* barked (perhaps because they were nowhere within fifty miles of this lovely hill resort in the Kumaon). No *ghoral* gave his alarm sneeze. No white-throated thrush chattered, no babblers babbled. All those denizens of the jungle who used to warn our childhood favourite, Jim Corbett, or Carpet Sahib, as the hill folk called him, were obviously absent on leave or had become friends with the panther. And despite the absence of this orchestrated warning from the jungle choir, he was very much present – old sinew, but still mean and malevolent. Just a serrating, scrabbling noise through the brush, the almost instinctive stampede of the unsuspecting herd, and the panther had his teeth around the neck of a cow. The hill cow, short and stunted, mooed and grunted and shook its head as if it couldn't believe what was going on; struggled, stumbled, and fell, but the panther kept his hold on the neck till the throes ceased and she lay still, her eyes bulging in terror and disbelief even in death.

Mime, as we all know, is a great art, the gesture often larger than the meaning it sets out to convey. Mime is graphic, as against words, which have a habit of getting soiled and cliched with overuse. In fact, mime has a head start over the word. A day later, Gangua mimed the entire episode in front of Mansab Ali. Arms outstretched – the wide road; arm pointed skywards to the west – the sun was very much up; then crawling on all fours and putting his hand in front of his eyes – and still the panther came stalking the herd, though Gangua never saw him. Then a leap in the air, eyes wide with anger. He mimed the panther roaring, showed how his mane rose in bristles at right angles to his neck, making him look much larger than he was. (There is an old belief in the hills that a panther doubles in size when he goes for the kill). And he produced the guttural sounds, both of the panther and the cow, and the way the panther shook it and carried it away, though he was too old to drag her very far. Mansab Ali asked, waving his arms double-fisted as if he was brandishing a lathi – did Gangua go for the panther with his stick? The boy smiled and shook his head. But he had yelled a lot – Gangua cupped his hands over his mouth and produced a loud hoarse sound; he hopped about and took a cup to his lips – he had run to the roadside tea stall for help.

The tea stall owner had, in turn, raised a din, but wisely enough, never left the side of his ever-boiling kettle. People gathered around slowly and eventually drove the old cat away after he had been at the kill for a while. A council was held. Once, after such an event, the villagers had smeared the dead calf with insecticide, and a panther, which had returned to the kill, had got poisoned and had moaned and roared around for three days before he had presumably died, though his carcass was never found. But better reason prevailed this time. No one wanted a repeat of that agonised moan to echo through the valley once again.

A few days later, to everyone's astonishment, they found the old panther lying still near a goat track. A villager had bolted at the sight but the cat made no attempt to follow him. People started throwing stones but Spotty never stirred. He was dead, of a heart attack, said Dr Kala, the town vet. Now people could have a good look at his maw. The village drunk, on whom the Devi descended on *ashtami*, was ridiculed, for no tooth was missing from the panther's jaw. There was much raillery and even the drunk's shamanistic credentials came under a cloud.

Panther or no panther, Gangua lost his job. People requested Shahji not to throw Gangua out. What more could the poor boy have done in the face of the panther's fury? He was just a cowherd and not a Bheem. But the acerbic Shahji would have none of it. Another *bagh* was sure to smell Gangua out, he said. A deaf mute in charge of the herd was a specific invitation to the panther. That winter in the warm kitchen, with woodsmoke swirling around them, the mime sessions between Mansab Ali and Gangua became longer. And Mansab grew so accustomed to this particular dialogue that when friends, or a benevolent dead aunt, or angels entered his dreams, their smiles were broad and they opened their arms wide to embrace him. And if, once in a while, his demons plagued him in his sleep, they never spoke, never reprimanded him. Only the wrinkles ran deeper, and the eyeballs rolled in their cavernous recesses. They distorted their faces and exaggerated their gestures; in a word, they mimed.

MY MAMMA NEVER CRIED

Kanika Gahlaut

If you see my Mamma's wedding pictures, nowhere will you find Mamma weeping into her hanky the way other people's Mammas do, their new husbands looking awkwardly on as they lower their *gota*-covered heads into the Ambassador car with red roses on the bonnet. Not my Mamma. She stared straight ahead at the lens, 'even during the *bidai*', she told me proudly once when I was going through the album with her (though she did say that her own Mamma, my *nani*, was alarmed by her lack of modesty and kept instructing her all through the wedding to lower her gaze).

But then, my Mamma never cried. During the yearly visit to Nani's, I would hear my maternal aunts talk as they sat on the *charpais* in the winter sun, their tones lowered so that the children couldn't hear, their knitting furious as they remembered Nina's first-born, my elder brother who had died even before I was born. 'But our Nina, she was always brave,' Aunty Anita would declare. Aunty Nita would nod in agreement and Nani would shake her head, silently grieving for her daughter.

Mamma didn't cry when Nani died either. She stood so quietly near the body wrapped in a *dupatta* that all the mourners went straight to Aunties Nina and Anita to offer condolence, bypassing Mamma, who was so composed in comparison that she could have passed as a curious neighbour.

It's not that Mamma didn't feel pain. If you heard the noise that came from my parents' bedroom when my handsome, amicable father, a captain in the Army, came home from work, changed into his shorts, downed a couple of rums and began beating her, you wouldn't have been left in any doubt that she must hurt. But even after the most extreme of beatings, when Mamma was exhausted from cowering in a corner for hours, trying to keep her ears and head safe so that the blows would not be fatal, she would just get up and get on with her life as if the beating was a household ritual, like the washing of clothes.

When I would creep into the house – as I grew older, I found a rather cowardly trick that worked better than trying to shut my ears to the sound of hand hitting back, foot hitting mouth, and would simply sneak out of the house and wander around in the garden, till I knew it was safe to go in – I would find my Mamma, usually in the kitchen, stacking away the dishes, and I would hug her and tell her that I loved her most in the world.

I liked to tell Mamma I loved her. It always led to an evening of stories between Mamma and I. Sometimes, we would go out into the verandah and look up at the sky for *Bhalu Bholeram*. We would then scout the skyline for 'the evil witch with the broomstick' and never find her. That's because – and I always told Mamma to tell me this part again – God had instructed *Bhalu Bholeram* to be the guardian and playmate in the sky of all the good people in the world, while all the bad people got *the witch*. 'So if you see *Bhalu Bholeram*, that means God loves you and has given orders to *Bhalu* to look after you,' she would say. And since *Bhalu* had special powers to make the wishes of his wards come true (while the witch didn't have any powers at all, which is why, in her frustration, she would periodically throw her broomstick around in the sky, causing numerous airplane crashes), I could ask for any wish I wanted. On other days, when Mamma would be too beaten up to do anything but sit in bed with me, I would fetch her photo album and she would turn the pages, telling me stories about Aunty Anita, Aunty Nita and her childhood in the village. She would become sad when she came to her father's pictures. 'If he hadn't died, I wouldn't have had to get married so early and I would have become an IAS officer,' she said once.

I asked her once if she had asked *Bhalu Bholeram* to make her an IAS officer, and she said she had forgotten. 'But I asked him for you, and he gave you to me,' she said. 'And if you become an IAS officer, I will be just as happy.'

I must have been six years old when my father got posted from Chandigarh to a Field Area near Ladakh, where the beatings began to get worse. One day, Mamma didn't get out of bed till two in the afternoon and when I went to her bedroom to wake her, I thought she was dead: her lip was cut, there was a gash above her left eyebrow and her eye wouldn't open, it was so swollen. The beatings got a lot worse before I found out I was the reason.

I sneaked into the house earlier than I generally did one day – partly because I was anxious to show Mamma my collection of particularly round plain *patthars* (pebbles) that I had been collecting all day (Mamma always evaluated the roundness of the pebbles, and when she found one to be near perfect, she would keep it and give me a shiny round fifty paisa in exchange, which I would put into my piggy bank). As I hesitated near the bedroom door, I heard Mamma plead with my father:

'But she has to resume her studies. How can she sit at home, she will lose precious years!'

'Teach her at home, you bitch. What did I get a bloody B.A.-educated wife for?'

'But she needs to go to a recognised school if we want her to get admission in a school of some repute when we get a posting to a big town.'

Father, of course, only answered in the way he knew best: with a repeated thud-thud-thud-thud that resounded around the house.

'Please, schools are very competitive these days. We could ruin her future.'

Thud-thud-thud-thud. Like the ayah pounding the clothes extra hard with the stick. Like plain *patthars* being slammed against each other, the sharpness of the noise muffled by cloth.

There was no school in the Field Area, and officers with children had the option of their families staying in a separate accommodation in a city. But my father would have none of it: he believed that a man's wife must stay with him and look after his needs.

After all, 'I have a long way to go in the army, and I couldn't possibly do it without my wife at my side,' he would always say with a wink, when he called colleagues over to our home, and they – with their own wives in New Delhi or Lucknow or with their parents – would compliment Mamma on the superb home-cooked food.

My Mamma wouldn't give up. She made friends with some wives of civilians in the area and found out there was a school in a nearby town: it wasn't a big school, in fact, my class – Standard 1 – would have only three children in it, but it was recognised by the Board. And as I was the child 'of an Army Officer and all, it would be a privilege to have her in our school', the principal told Mamma when she went to meet him in the morning one day while Father was at work. 'In fact, no problem, Madam, we have no problem in admitting her in the class even though three months of syllabus is already over,' he said, his toupee bobbing with enthusiasm. 'I am sure, being from a family like yours, she will catch up with her classmates in no time.'

Actually, it took another month of constant pleadings on Mamma's part, beatings from my father and fervent requests to *Bhalu Bholeram* on my part – more because I wanted the beatings to stop than because I particularly understood the importance of an education – before it was finally arranged for me to leave for the school in a *jonga* that my father asked for from his office, a request to which his seniors immediately agreed.

It was another two months before Mamma found out what was happening in school. I didn't want to tell her, I promise. Not that I didn't think of telling her. Sometimes, I would even make up my mind on the *jonga* ride back home that I would blurt it out. But then I would see the look on her face when she greeted me at the door, extending her arm for the satchel with Mickey Mouse on it – which she had asked Aunty Anita to send especially for me all the way from New Delhi – and telling me what she had cooked for lunch (lunch was always our favourite meal, just Mamma and I, because Father would still be in office and took a tiffin), and I would somehow lose my nerve.

'So how was school, *beta*?' Mamma would ask at the dining table.

'Good, Mamma.'

'Good or very good?'

'Very good, Mamma.'

'What did you learn today, *beta*?'

'I learnt how to write an essay in the English class. Mrs Khatri is very nice.'

'And what did you learn in the math class?'

Math class.

I hated math. And I always failed the weekly tests, much to the surprise of my other two classmates (both boys), considering that I was clearly Sir's favourite.

Sir, with his oily hair leaving a damp mark on the collar of his shirt and his habit of saying two-plus-two in such a vehement manner that you had to turn your head to escape the spit, would always make me sit next to him.

Lately, I had begun to feel ill before the math class. My heart would pound and I would feel a sinking feeling in my stomach when the bell announced the start of the third period, Math. Sir had begun to hold the classes sitting at the back of the room. He would write the sums on the blackboard, then take his seat at the back and ask the class to complete the sums in half an hour. He would then casually call out to me and ask me to sit next to him while I completed my sums. While the other two were bent over their sums, his hand found its way up my uniform frock, his chalky fingers leaving a white smudge on the navy blue hem. My finger would grip the pencil tightly and my hands would sweat.

Finally, I didn't have to tell Mamma. One day she came into my class during the English period and the English teacher said, 'Good morning Madam, I have been waiting for you.' Mamma gave the other children a bag of sweets, after asking for permission from Teacher. 'Is everything okay, Mrs Khatri?' Mamma asked pleasantly, but I knew Mamma was tense from the way she kept pushing back a strand of her hair. 'Madam, I think we should go outside to talk,' said Mrs Khatri. She told us to open to page 4 of the grammar book and turned to Mamma. 'I saw something the other day which made me very concerned, Madam, which I should tell you about, but please, it is to remain confidential or I will lose my job ...' I heard her say as she took Mamma outside.

Mamma came back fifteen minutes later and told me to get my satchel. All through the journey, Mamma was quiet. I could not bear the silence any longer. I turned to her and put my face in her lap. 'I am sorry Mamma,' I blurted out, believing that Mamma must be angry with me.

That was the first time I ever saw my Mamma cry.

NINE-NUMBER BUNGALOW

Sunny Singh

Death came silently, frequently, to the little community in the mountains. And it always chose the men. They would go away on mysterious journeys, on *operations*, carrying olive green rucksacks and black weapons glistening with oil like a schoolgirl's plaits. Fingers caressed prayer beads, lips moved soundlessly over the sacred words, and eyes looked steadily forward.

Left behind, the women would watch the trucks disappear into the distance. And a little later, the hum of a plane would rise from the distant airstrip. They would pause in their conversations, their prayers, their cooking, to hear the hum grow softer as the aeroplane flew far, far away.

Theirs was a small community, spread over a mountainside, dotted with bungalows that the British had built nearly a century ago. Lower down the slopes were the barracks, and still lower and closest to the plains, the tiny market place. Beyond the deodar tops, the mountainside dipped into a wide valley – the Doon valley – with its soil rich with fragrant basmati scents, the many lights of Dehra twinkling at night.

On clear nights, lights twinkled across the valley, on the mountains at its other end, like a sparkling necklace flung carelessly across the heights. That necklace, where sirens never called for black-outs, was Mussoorie, a tourist town, a social, partying, happy town. Even as a seven year old, Ruchi knew, when she watched the Mussoorie lights, that Death went infrequently to that far town.

Death stayed right here in her cantonment town, stalking through the misty mountain top above the bungalows, where multi-coloured prayer flags fluttered, sneaking past the offices where the *operations* were planned, creeping past the cheerful barracks smelling of butter tea, *thukpa*, *momos*, and human determination. Death climbed secretly on to the olive green trucks that carried the men away on operations. It stowed away on the aeroplanes that flew the men even farther than the Doon valley below.

Ruchi knew this because when the men returned, grim and weary, there would be faces missing in their ranks. 'Death marched again with us,' her father, unshaven and bone tired, would inform her mother as he collapsed on the soft bed, too weary to even remove his mud-spattered jungle boots. Mother would look grave, sometimes even weep a little, as she removed Father's boots and then tucked him safe under the vast green down-quilt.

When Death took the officers, their passing would be marked with a quick, sombre toast at the Mess, and hasty removal of the dead man's family down to the plains. In the barracks, the passing was even quieter. A face would vanish to be replaced by another impassive, slant-eyed one, even as the other soldiers continued their chanting: '*Om Mani Padme Om.*'

* * *

On days when Father was not away on operations, he took

Ruchi for walks on the mountainside. They would walk through the deodars, rhododendrons, and pines on the higher reaches. Ruchi's favourite stretch was a dim path lined with towering pine trees, where the ground was carpeted by tangy smelling needles that sank under her feet. In the dim twilight that always lived under the tall trees, Father taught her to walk silently, testing the twigs and needles under her soft-soled shoes. 'Not a crack,' he would instruct, solemnly demonstrating his own stealth. Later, kneeling on the pine-needle carpet in companionable silence, they would watch the clouds swirl through the narrow gaps in the mountains and observe the furry creatures of the forest go about their own business.

Once, while walking on the soft pine carpet, Ruchi found a small furry body the colour of dry dirt. A faint, acrid smell rose from it. 'Death marched with it,' Father murmured, running his fingers through her hair and pulling her head close to his body. They moved away, Father carrying her back home in his arms. From the edge of their garden overlooking the pine walk, Ruchi watched him instruct one of the soldiers. 'Bury the body, *pinja-la*, I don't want her upset again,' he said, holding Ruchi tight in his arms.

Later, when Father went to the offices near the top of the hill, Ruchi ran down to the pine walk to see the animal again. The body was gone, the patch covered with a fresh layer of sharp, green needles. But the odour of the non-living still lingered on the spot, blending with the fresh, sharp scent of the pines.

* * *

When she grew older, Ruchi could never remember how she came to identify Nine-number bungalow as Death's house. Perhaps Gompo-la, the sweet-tempered soldier-monk who watched over her as she played, informed her. Or perhaps Father told her about the abandoned old house with a faded number nine painted in black on its rickety wooden gate, that stood not half a kilometre from their own.

Its red roof was of the same corrugated metal as the other bungalows. Its wide veranda had the same wide wooden floorboards. The front of the house had a large picture window, with even, square windowpanes set in an ornate rosewood frame. But unlike other bungalows, the paint was peeling off the yellowed walls; the red on the roof had faded. Even the rosewood didn't shine with fresh polish. The garden was overgrown with weeds covering the pebbled path. The rose bushes were twisted and gnarled with age, and the wild irises flashed a startlingly bright blue in the tall grass.

She did, however, remember the first time she walked up to Nine-number bungalow, so similar to her own. With Father. They had gone to the bungalow for cloud-catching.

The clouds on the mountains never came low enough to enter her bungalow. Instead, they swirled and twisted and blanketed the mountain-top with foamy pearl grey. 'We are too low, Ruchi,' Father would explain patiently. On such days, when the mountain-top was hidden by the clouds, Father would take her up to let her run through the prayer flags, tasting the moisture on her tongue, trailing cloud-phantoms at the tips of her fingers.

She would run through the clouds, letting the damp, wispy yet opaque streams hide her. And then, she would wait for Father to find her. 'Ruchi,' Father would call, striding through the translucence, cutting through the clouds. 'Ruchi,' he would call again, laughter audible in his voice. And then he would appear through the clouds, large and solid amidst the vapours, like a hero, or a god – his hair slicked and shiny with the moisture, his cheeks cold with the mountain air. Laughing, he would swoop down to gather Ruchi in his arms, his clothes damp and cold. But his arms were warm and strong. He would carry her home, marching steadily out of the clouds.

But she had wanted to trap the clouds. To catch them

inside the house, and keep them forever. She wanted to open the windows to let the clouds come into the rooms. And then quickly, very quickly, just when they filled the rooms, she would close the windows. And the clouds would have to stay in the house for her to play with, whenever she wanted.

When Ruchi explained her plan to Father, he had laughed. But when he stopped laughing, he patted her head. 'A good plan, a very good plan. Like a guerrilla's. You are learning fast.'

'So I can go on operations with you soon?' Ruchi immediately asked. That was the whole point of showing Father that clouds could be caught; that her tactics were as good as any officer's; that she was ready to be a guerrilla like the *pinja-las*.

'Hmm, soon! Let me see. I think you have to be a little taller to be a guerrilla,' Father solemnly informed her, examining her closely, holding his palm a little above her head – the height he explained was necessary to be a guerrilla. 'But we should test your plan for trapping the clouds. Very good plan. We won't hold them forever, but just as a test. For a little while only. Alright?'

The only hitch of course was that their own home was too low for the clouds to reach. The only bungalow high enough to lure the clouds was Nine-number bungalow. Death's house.

Father said that he would find a good time to go up to the bungalow. Ruchi knew he would watch for a time when Death had gone walking. Then they would sneak in and work at cloud-catching.

It was many days later that Father decided the time was right. The sky was dark and when he walked with Ruchi through the deodars, the wind blew fierce and cold, sucking away her breath and stinging her cheeks.

Hand in hand, they approached the gaping, blind windows. The glass panes were dirty and dim, but no curtains hid the empty insides. As she placed her foot on the first wooden step to the veranda, the board creaked, moaning softly under her feet. She froze immediately, holding her breath. Father smiled at her, pointing to his own feet that stepped cunningly, silently on the same boards. She nodded, shifting her weight carefully to not make a sound with her next step.

The door was bolted but not locked. When Father tugged at the bolt, it squealed loudly. Ruchi's heart gave a lurch. What if the sound had warned Death? But Father just smiled and that reassured her.

Once inside, Father and Ruchi sped through the rooms, flinging the windows open, careful not to make a sound. Latches protested, frames creaked, but they continued. 'Look, they are on their way down,' Father pointed out at the picture window. Ruchi turned her head to see the clouds roll down from the top of the mountain. Like spreading rolls of silk, or a flood, the clouds made their way down, covering the tall pines and deodars. Steadily, almost imperceptibly, the first translucent fingers would reach to caress a tree, then slowly wrap themselves around the green heights. And moments later, the tree would be invisible, hidden in the voluminous grey blanket.

Watching the clouds make their way inexorably through the forest, down the mountains, Ruchi felt a flash of terror. A cold, wet finger ran fleetingly down her spine, raising the soft hair on the back of her neck. Her stomach churned, and her breath caught in her throat. Suddenly the mist seemed sinister, portending evil in a way it never had on the mountaintop.

Beside her, Father laughed, throwing his head back. 'We'll catch them alright.' Ruchi had a sudden vision of the mysterious operations he went away for. The enemy approached, much like the clouds, vast and strong and sinister. And hidden with the *pinja-las* in their posts, their gleaming weapons loaded and ready, her father laughed in anticipation.

That cold wet finger on her spine, she realised in a flash of frighteningly adult clarity, was her fear for her father. Her stomach had churned with that terrifying intuition that all those who love a soldier must learn to live with. Death marched with her father too, and at any moment, at any place, could swoop down to claim him. She felt tears prick her eyes, even as the clouds reached the house, swirling gently against the peeling yellowed walls.

'Stay here,' Father commanded, laughter still in his voice. 'I'll go close the windows.' Ruchi could only make a sound, a clutching sob that ripped at her throat as Father moved away. She reached out after him but caught only a damp wisp. The clouds had already started crowding Death's bungalow, pushing through the picture window like unruly children at recess.

Already blinded by the billowing opacity, she could hear Father closing the windows, bolting each one carefully. She strained to hear his footsteps, but he walked as ever on soundless feet. Time seemed to have halted, and nothing moved in the clouds that had filled the house. She held out her hands before her and could only vaguely make out their outline.

Ruchi stared at the damp blindness around her, and felt an unidentifiable terror clutch at her heart. Tears now poured down her cheeks. Her hands were cold and clammy with the moisture from the clouds. She rested her head against the rosewood frame, finding solace in its solidity, and sobbed uncontrollably.

She didn't hear Father return. She was staring blindly before her when the figure loomed silently over her. The shoulders were massive, the head dark. It leaned out to pull one of the panels of the picture window shut. Ruchi held her breath, hoping that it wouldn't notice her. Then the figure seemed to search for something, the dark, slim-fingered hands running over the rosewood window frame. She hid in her corner, shrinking within herself in fear. Oh, if only Father would return!

As the hands moved closer, she closed her eyes, squeezing them shut. She screamed when the hand touched her shoulder. 'No!'

Then suddenly she was in Father's arms, cradled against his chest. 'What frightened you, baby? It's alright, everything is alright,' he murmured against her hair. His lips felt her cheeks, passing over the tears and the moisture the clouds had left. 'Shhh, it's alright.'

He carried her home just like that, holding her head nestled under his chin, her body pressed tight against his chest. She could feel his pulse throbbing in his throat against her face and pressed tight against the rhythm. 'He is alive, he is still alive,' she exulted, breathing in his scent – musky and tangy like the forest. She knew she was echoing words in her mind that she had heard her mother whisper each time Father came home. They were a chant, a sacred chant, like *Om Mani Padme Om*. Suddenly, she knew what the chant meant, why the *pinja-la* chanted it as they went on operations. 'He is alive, he is still alive.'

And the first inklings of a plan began to form in her head, as she pressed herself closer still to Father.

She would imprison Death; leave him locked in his Nine-number bungalow before Father left again on operations. She would make sure that Death would never march again with the soldiers.

* * *

The day before Father left on operations, he always spoke to Ruchi separately. The words were different each time, but the message was always the same.

They would walk down to the shaded pine-walk, hand in hand, walking carefully on the needles. 'You must take care of Mother. She worries too much. So you must be brave and take care of her.' Ruchi always nodded seriously and held Father's hand tighter. They would slowly walk back home.

The night before Father left, there was always a big dinner with all his favourite dishes. And Mother made a special treat:

ice cream packed with raisins, wild berries picked from the bushes on the slope and shreds of tangy-sweet plums from the tree in the garden. The three of them would sit together over dinner, talking softly about unimportant things such as a new doll for Ruchi, or Mom's demand for a new pressure cooker. Sitting up so late, Ruchi would almost fall asleep on the table. Unlike other days, she wasn't told to go to bed.

Later, Father would carry her to bed and tuck her in. He would stroke her forehead softly and kiss her cheek. Ruchi knew that on the nights before he left, Father stayed up late to talk to Mother. She would lie half-asleep in her bed, listening to the murmurs from the next room, the rustling of sheets and the incomprehensible, hushed moans that came from her parents' room. At some point, as she tried to make sense of the sounds, she would fall asleep.

In the morning, when she awoke, Father would have left already.

Which is why she needed to carry out her Death-trapping plan before Father took her for a stroll to the pine-walk. She had already heard the murmurs, listening in secretly to the things that adults said at dinners in the officers' mess when they thought the children couldn't hear.

'High casualties on the eastern sector .... four companies decimated... full war this time ... Major Rai and his boys just cut down at the dam ... poor Mrs Rajan, after only one month of marriage, he has been sent on ops ...'

Mother had already told me that Father would be gone for a long time. 'This time, the operations may last a long time, Ruchi. But maybe we will go down to the plains and see your cousins. We can even go to Nani's house.' But Mother had tears in her eyes as she said this and Ruchi knew that Death would march with Father and his men on this trip.

But she wouldn't let that happen.

For days, she had thought of a plan. She had carefully examined the lock on the big trunk under the bed. It was the only lock in the house, a big shiny yellow lock, with a dull steel handle. And its key – in a large round ring with lots of other keys – stayed in the top drawer of the high mahogany dresser in her parents' bedroom.

She had tried to take the shiny brass key out from the ring. The ring held other keys too. The whole bunch was very heavy and loud too, clanking with every movement. But the ring was tight, its spirals almost impossible to prise apart. In the end, she took the whole bunch, deciding to return it after she had locked Death in.

Removing the lock from the trunk under the bed had been easier. Mother knew that Ruchi often played under the bed and never disturbed her. 'She is afraid,' Mother had told Father, 'it is this uncertainty all around.' But the lock was heavy, making her arms ache when she carried it – with both hands – up the mountain. The keys clanged loudly in her pocket.

'Baba, where are you going?' Gompo-la called after her. She nearly cried in frustration at being spotted. He caught up with her easily, loping after her with his long stride. For a moment, she hesitated.

'To Nine-number bungalow,' she whispered, unable to lie to the concerned face above her.

Gompo-la was surprised. 'But no one goes there, Ruchi baba.'

'Oh, I know,' she declared airily, trying to hide the lock behind her back. Gompo-la had already seen the lock. He didn't ask any more questions. Instead, he squatted down before her, balancing on the balls of his feet, waiting for her explanation. Ruchi stared at him, wondering if he would laugh at her, or worse, stop her from carrying out her plan.

Finally, she decided. 'I am going to lock Death in the house. Then he can't march with the soldiers tomorrow. It's a secret and you have to help me.'

Gompo-la seemed surprised. But he didn't laugh. Or even ask any questions. He nodded wisely, his narrow eyes suddenly shiny and moist. 'In the old days, in Tibet, we did the same. Before a war, the lamas locked away all the evil spirits. Come, I will help you.'

So, they walked hand in hand up to Nine-number bungalow. Gompo-la volunteered to go and find out if Death indeed was home. As he sneaked up through the garden, Ruchi watched the silent house. Its windows were bolted shut again. From a distance, she thought she saw a shadow move inside. Scared, she huddled down further, clutching the lock tightly.

Then Gompo-la came back. 'Yes, he is here. Give me the lock, I will go put it on the door.' He held out his hand. But she shook her head. Only she knew the secret words. Or rather, the meaning of the sacred words that had to be said after she locked Death in.

'No, I have to put the lock myself.'

Gompo-la nodded again, his eyes shining brightly. 'Good officer always do first what he asks the *jawans* to do,' he said, stepping aside.

Ruchi rose slowly to her feet, inching forward towards the house. Before her, the silent bungalow loomed large and frightening. The sun glinted off the window panes and she wondered if Death had seen her approach. The pebbles rolled and crunched under her feet; the weeds scratched her bare legs as she forced herself to walk steadily up to the front door.

Once she stumbled as she walked. She put her hands out before her. She didn't fall but hit her hands against the pebbles. The lock was heavy and crushed her fingers as she touched the ground. There would be scratches, but when she looked down at her hands, there was no blood. One of her hands, however, had touched a scorpion-grass plant at her feet, and began to itch. She felt tears well up in her eyes and forced herself not to wipe them off. The poisonous grass would make her eyes burn too if she took her hand up to them.

She looked back and Gompo-la was still crouching on the ground beyond the garden. He smiled at her and motioned her forward, swinging his right arm in a high, wide arc. She nodded and gathered her courage. She would tolerate the itching and the pain until she got back. Then Gompo-la would find the plants to take the hurt away.

The first step up to the veranda began to creak before she remembered what Father had taught her. She removed her foot and then replaced it slowly, shifting her weight to tread silently. Silently, slowly, almost holding her breath, she climbed up to the veranda.

Swiftly stepping across the wide floorboards, she reached the door. Fumbling, nearly dropping the lock, she struggled to place it on the loop of the bolt. The door shook suddenly, banging against the frame, pulling away from her hands. Was someone trying to open it from the inside? She started, her heart beating wildly and half turned to run away. But then, she steadied herself, reaching for the bunch of keys in her pocket.

Concentrating fiercely, she found the shiny brass key, the only one in the bunch, and managed to fit it into the lock. '*Om Mani Padme Om,*' she chanted under her breath, using all the strength in her arms to twist the key in the slot. The key was stuck and refused to move. She jiggled it in the lock, tugging at it, struggling to turn it. Finally, she felt the lock click shut. She tugged at it once, twice, before removing the key. For an instant, it caught in the lock again, and she had to twist it before it snapped free.

Triumphant, she turned, holding the key up for Gompo-la to see. He jumped up and waved and laughed. She thought she knew what Father felt when his operations were over. Taking a deep breath, stifling the urge to run away from the house, she climbed steadily down the steps, through the garden and out on to the path. 'Well done, baba, well done,' Gompo-la shouted. As she drew closer, he smiled at her solemnly and stuck out his hand. Ruchi took it in hers, shaking it as she had seen Father do with his officers. 'Thank you for your help on this mission, Gompo-la,' she intoned her father's words, mimicking his tone.

Gompo-la smiled and nodded, a different gesture this time. It was a crisp duck of the head, an almost-salute that the guerrillas used to acknowledge each other. Then, he bent down and put his hands on her shoulders. 'Very good,' he announced, looking solemnly, deeply into her eyes. Ruchi was glad that his hands were strong because her legs were shaking with the pent-up fear and relief. He smelled different from Father, of sweat and cigarettes and of cooked meats from the kitchen. For a long moment, he stared at her, his eyes inscrutable. Then releasing her shoulders, he stepped back, rose and clicked his heels together. She looked up to see his wide grin.

Without a word, she held out her hands to him and he leaned over to inspect them, noting the red itchy rash that had sprung up on her fingers. 'No problem. Behind our house, there are plants that will stop the itching. You will be tip-top by the time we reach home,' he announced.

When she looked up at him, he was smiling. She laughed out loud, joyously, relieved; a laugh so infectious that he joined in. Laughing, they began their walk back down the mountain.

* * *

When Ruchi awoke the next morning, Father had left on operations. She ate in silence and then found a seat on the veranda, the place where she always sat to wait for his return. She knew it would be some days before Father came home, but she watched the road twisting down the hill anyway. And softly, under her breath, she chanted.

The sun was high in the sky when Gompo-la came, having finished his chores, and sat on the steps, next to her stool. They smiled at each other conspiratorially. Watching the road together, they began to chant the sacred words, the words of hope:

Om Mani Padme Om!
He is alive. He is still alive.
Om Mani Padme Om …

THE BICYCLE THIEF

Pramod Kapoor

In those days courtyards were very important to a house. The size and number of courtyards reflected the social status of its occupants. I spent my childhood living in just such a house of courtyards in Benares. Made up of seven courtyards of varying sizes, our house was called Dewan Saheb ki Haveli. Family partition, over generations, had changed its size, face and social value. Of the seven huge courtyards, my immediate family was left with only one. The east and north sides of this courtyard were occupied by my father and his widowed sister. The south side lay deserted and somewhat close to being a ruin. I think family disputes prevented repair and maintanence, but as children we were asked to leave whenever animated discussions took place over the ownership of this part. The courtyard was the most happening place. Marriages, *mundans*, deaths – all the ceremonies took place here.

My grandfather's dead body was kept in the centre of this courtyard for an entire night because Baba, my father, was in Calcutta when he died. Poor Dadi, she was brought to the courtyard three times almost dead, with Ma whispering verses from the *Ramayana* into her ear, in anticipation that she would go to heaven listening to sacred verses. All three times she survived and was taken back to her bed.

We knew very little of the Guruji who lived on the west side except that he was much respected, cutting across the family friction and often settling minor disputes between feuding siblings. Despite my young age I could not escape noticing a family resemblance in his appearance. This was often the topic of discussion among the neighbours. Guruji had his own group of *bhajan* singers. They met several times a week to sing reverant songs as offerings to Devi. I enjoyed their music and was often allowed in the chorus. But to me, stealing sweet *prasad* from Guruji's small little wooden cabinet, was more thrilling. For fear of reprimand I did not dare to share the sweets even with my little sister with whom I played all day. Whenever sweets were found missing, the family knew who would have eaten them. I had the sweetest tooth in the entire neighbourhood.

If stealing sweets gave me thrills, exploring the deserted southside was a greater adventure. Apart from a small store of cooking coal which we were told was full of snakes, the other two rooms housed wasted heirlooms. From ornate door knobs, to broken pieces of sculpture, to prayer bells and other wares – the two rooms were like toy stores to me. But among all these treasures what I liked the most was a trunk full of 78 rpm records. The trunk had the best *dadra* and *thumris* sung by Badi Kashi Bai, Moti Bai, Jaddan Bai and the best of the time. The colourful labels in the centre of the records fascinated me the most. One day I selected five of my favourite colours to seek further adventure. I lit two candles, brought one of the records close to the flame and to my utter delight it started to curve. I felt as if I had invented something with which I could finally make my family happy and proud. The next day I turned one of the Jaddan Bai records into a flower vase. Much to my dismay Ma shouted and slapped me and threatened to report this to Baba. I felt my great piece of creativity was beyond Ma's understanding and decided to give the vase to our neighbour's little daughter, who really loved it.

I wasn't very popular among the neighbours. In the height of summer, when the entire neighbourhood was enjoying its afternoon siesta, I would knock on doors to call other children to play cricket in the lane. The deserted lane in the hot summer afternoon made a great cricket field. Being the best built I would show off and hit the ball hard and break the neighbouring windows. If summer afternoon was a great time for cricket for me, it was also the season for many fights between the Dewani lane neighbourhood. After every fight I would promise Ma never to play again with the children of those wretched neighbours but somehow I could never sleep through the hot summer winds. The furious sound of the wind hitting the window pane was too enticing to remain in bed. The thought of a cricket game in the deserted lane would make me forget my promise. And more importantly I was a hero to my mates and I took my leadership rather seriously.

It was one such Sunday afternoon and as usual I was restless in bed. It was past lunch. Baba had brought some delicious *langra* mangoes and after the habitual heavy Sunday lunch, all of us had our fill of mangoes. Baba and his friends were discussing the varieties of *langra* and how this year the yield of the finest variety from Rani ka Bagh was so small that practically nothing had reached the *mandi*. I was getting bored and impatient with this mundane discussion, and desperately wanted to slip out when everyone had dozed off to sleep. I made my first attempt half an hour later. But I was caught and dragged back to the room which was darkened by the wet curtain of *khus*, which was used to keep the room cool.

I was still very restless and as soon as I heard Baba's first serious snore, I thought it was safe to escape. The risk was high. It was to be my second attempt and if I was caught this time, it wouldn't just be a shouting or a slap. Baba would certainly debar me from playing cricket the entire summer and worse still, he might decide not to take me with him to see the test match in Kanpur's Green Park the following winter. Yet the temptation was too high. I would lose my superiority among the boys if I failed to show up in the lane. It was worth taking the risk. So instead of going down the steps on foot, I decided to slide down on my backside!

No sooner had I reached the last step leading to the courtyard, than Baba thundered 'Premoo'. I froze and in that frozen moment I yelled back 'Thief! Thief! Catch him! Catch him!' Baba came running down and soon the entire household had gathered around the courtyard. Servants, my brothers, the guests, and also the lawyer who lived next door. In the middle of the courtyard the bicycle lay flat as if someone had just thrown it away in fright. Everyone came rushing to the lane, which moments ago, would have been our exclusive cricket pitch. I pointed to a man I thought was trying to steal the bicycle. I was in complete shock as everyone was reacting too swiftly and being the cause of the chaos, I had to respond to them. I do not know if someone was indeed making an attempt to steal. Was it Baba's yell that made me shout? Was it the fear of being caught escaping for the second time? Or did I shout to divert attention? Honestly I do not know. I was too scared. But the cycle was not in its usual parking space. It lay flat in the courtyard. At the time, the only explanation to me was that someone must have made an attempt to steal! Lawyer Uncle insisted that we must report this to the police. 'Today it's a bicycle,' he exclaimed, 'who knows tomorrow it could be anything, may be the expensive utensils which are left in the courtyard after being washed.'

On Lawyer Uncle's advice a police complaint was registered and I was made to identify the thief from a group of six or seven men who were paraded in the court. I was all of five and I remember Lawyer Uncle lifting me in his lap in the court so that the judge could see me. Ignoring Lawyer Uncle's foul and sweaty smell, I identified a man I had seen pass by the lane many times. He was called Lala. On being identified he was sent to jail. I don't know for how long but I know he was fined and convicted.

Baba was building a house on the outskirts of the city for a cleaner environment and greener living. A couple of weeks after the cycle incident, we moved out of the Haveli to our new house. Dadi died there. She always wanted to die in the house built for her by her son. I was greatly pained by her death. I thought she had had to pay for the sin I had committed by sending an innocent man to jail. After all she could have enjoyed the new house for a few years more. I would hear many stories of the Lala who had been jailed for stealing the bicycle. All full of miseries. Some said his wife died of tuberculosis while he was in prison. His children were thrown out of their school and that he was sacked by the *bania* he worked for. I was full of remorse. For many months whenever I saw pain and suffering in the family, I attributed it to the sin I had committed.

My own position in school slipped. I was often punished in front of the entire class for no mistake of mine. Perhaps much like the way I had made an innocent suffer for no mistake of his. Guruji suddenly got very sick and stopped singing *bhajans*; Baba had to close one of his shops; the family parrot died of no apparent reason, and Nani asked Ma not to send me to Calcutta that summer. I was told Nani was getting old and couldn't handle my naughtiness. And to top it all, the cricket tour of England was cancelled. This year we wouldn't go for our annual cricket picnic to Green Park in Kanpur. I had heard elders say that miseries come wholesale – all at one time. I didn't know one had to pay so dearly for just one sin. Many a time I thought of putting an end to my life but couldn't go beyond writing a suicide note. I would write these notes with great passion but would abandon the idea of suicide by the time I finished writing them. I thought the next best thing would be to run away from home. Perhaps my family wouldn't have to suffer for the wrong done by me. This time I didn't destroy the parting note and left it on the dressing table, the most prominent place in my parents' room, hoping in my heart of hearts that Ma would see it and get me back before I went too far. I was nabbed an hour later. Throughout this one hour, I kept looking for known faces, hoping that someone would recognise me and take me back to the house. I didn't really want to run away.

A year later I was sent to Calcutta for schooling. The new surroundings brought a lot of excitement. Nani's food was better cooked. Nana's hookah was even better. I almost choked the first time I tried it. I sucked the water instead of smoke. At school I was recognised as a better cricketer, chosen the class monitor because of my superior skills in mathematics and perhaps also my better built. By the time I left school to join St. Xaviers College I was the school captain and decorated as being the finest all-round student. Life in the last fifteen years had indeed taken a turn for the better. It landed me in the United States of America at the age of twenty-one. God, it seems, had forgiven me and with the passage of time the memory of the bicycle thief and the guilt I carried gradually faded.

Two years later and a little less wiser with regard to women, I married Wendy, two years my senior. We had two beautiful daughters. We made several trips to India visiting friends and family in Benares and Calcutta. It wasn't until the daughters were in their teens that I decided it was time we took them to Benares on an extended vacation to show them the city where I grew up. In Benares I would tell my family of my escapades and show them the places associated with my childhood. I was enjoying the nostalgia the city evoked in me and it was wonderful to share it with my family. It was during one such discussion that I volunteered to show them the old Haveli.

Wendy and the daughters were quite excited. They would

finally get to see the Haveli which had so frequently figured in the stories they had heard about Benares. For me too, this would be a very special trip. I was looking forward to seeing whether Ramu Halwai still made those delicious *jalebis*, and if Kallu Mochi would recognise me; to discover what had become of Nathu Darzi, the tailor who stitched all those smart school dresses for me. I remembered how I would always tell him to make patch pockets on my shorts. They looked smart and different from those of the other children. He used to get so irritated when I took the shorts every second day to stitch back the torn patch pockets. Didn't he warn me not to get those pockets!

As I approached the Haveli I saw how things had changed. Ramu Halwai didn't make *jalebis* in the open. Instead they were brought on a plate from the kitchen. He had turned his shop into a corner snack bar. Kallu Mochi had moved to another city after his son got a job in a shoe factory. Nathu Darzi had passed away leaving the shop to his two sons who thought they would make more money by selling the shop than stitching clothes their entire lifetime. The shop had become a doctor's clinic. But when we reached Dewan Saheb ki Haveli I felt nothing much had changed. The Haveli stood as it was when I had seen it last. The lane needed no repairs, and the windows had the same old green paint; the paint had cracked a bit.

As I started to make enquiries about third and fourth cousins about whom I had heard but never met or seen, a bearded man came out of a door six or seven houses away. My heart missed a beat. This is what I had feared. Although I had made a connection instantly when I saw him come out of the door, I didn't want to recognise him. He looked exactly like Lala the bicycle thief. Perhaps it was his son.

As he stepped forward and muttered something, I turned my back to him and told Wendy and the daughters to hurry. I didn't want to stay there anymore. 'We must rush home,' I told Wendy. 'There are so many people waiting for tea.' I was quiet and didn't say a word on our way back to the rickshaw. I kept thinking about Lala. He must be dead by now. Or was it he who had sent his son to insult me in front of my family? I wouldn't know and I didn't want to know. I didn't want to relive those painful memories which had haunted my childhood. I just wanted to turn away. Life had treated me so well since then. Why should I go through those painful memories which had now become mere regrettable pauses in my life?

But unaware of that painful part of my life, Wendy and the daughters kept insisting that we turn back and go into the Haveli. My younger daughter asked why I wanted to avoid the bearded man. He looked so friendly. Perhaps he was one of those many cousins we had never met. 'He could have told us so many stories of your childhood,' added Wendy. 'Perhaps those you do not remember or have forgotten to tell us about.'

I had no choice but to return. Irritated at the thought of seeing the bearded man, I said I would go back on one condition. We would go straight into the Haveli, meet our nearest cousins and leave in half an hour. And that's exactly what we did.

I was quite relieved not to see the bearded man on our return to the Haveli. But as we were about to step out of the main gate, he appeared again. Somehow this time I knew I couldn't get away and so made no attempt to avoid or walk away from him.

He came up to me with folded hands and asked if I was from Dewan Sahib's family. As I nodded my head I could see Lala, the bicycle thief, in him. This man was certainly his son. Looking at Wendy and the daughters he asked me if I was the same man who had migrated to America many years ago. While I nodded, I knew the moment of truth was near. My heart was pounding hard and my daughter who was holding my hand, could feel the sweat on my palm.

'I am Lala's son. Do you remember him?' Despite the sharp voice, the words were getting lost on me; they surfaced in intervals; moments were divided between what was happening now and what had happened on that fateful day. For one moment I was transported to that court scene many years ago when I had pointed at Lala to identify him. Yet, here and now, I was muttering to this bearded man, 'Yes, how is Lala?' I heard myself say, 'Yes, I do remember.' Totally irrelevant words desperately trying to find an escape for a trapped and guilty man.

'My father led a very honest life … he died a few weeks ago … never cheated anybody, let alone stealing from a neighbour … before he died he told me the only blemish in his life … the jail … he suffered a lot because of that one incident … his life changed thereafter … forever … you know what I am talking about … he was sent to jail for stealing your bicycle … that's not true … the truth is there was an emergency … my mother was dying … tuberculosis … he needed the bicycle to rush and get medicines for her … he was not a bicycle thief.'

For me that moment in time froze forever.

AFTERWORD

Ruskin Bond

When I heard that a galaxy of well-known writers and journalists was descending on, or ascending to Landour and Mussoorie, I was filled with some trepidation. Not that I am averse to the company of my own kind – far from it – but this literary jamboree was to be called a Festschrift, and I had no idea what the word meant; I still have difficulty in spelling and pronouncing it.

At first, I thought a festschrift implied some sort of orgy. And having, some twenty-five years ago, been hauled into a Mumbai court for writing an allegedly obscene short story, I felt a little apprehensive. Would a festschrift involve taking our clothes off, as in a masonic initiation ritual? Would I have to dance in my night-shirt, and that too on a cold April evening? Would we all have the vigour, and the figures for it? Certainly not I, nor our genial host, Pramod Kapoor of Roli Books. We'd have been given short shrift had we turned out in our festive slips.

I need not have worried. The participants were all normal

people. Correction. Writers are, by their very natures, abnormal people; I meant to say that they were civilised. Good-looking too. Especially some of those pretty young journalists. Just what the doctor had said would be good for my blood-pressure. And although we did cavort around a bonfire, it was with plenty of clothing on, for the Landour nights are cold at this time of the year.

It was a happy experience meeting other writers, most of whom have contributed stories to this volume. Many have already achieved distinction in their various fields. In our meetings we spoke of many things – literary critics, publishers, editors, ghosts, ghost writers, awards, rewards, translations: there was no dearth of subjects for discussion and argument. Between sessions we ate and drank, visited cemeteries, gazed at the homes of local celebrities (wishing we could have houses like theirs), wandered about the corridors of the old Savoy hotel (where a leopard-cat had gouged a hole in the cloth of the billiard-table), and shared our dreams. Friendships were made, and, so far as I know, none were broken.

When it was time for everyone to leave, I noticed tears in one or two eyes, including our host's. He put it down to sinus trouble, but I know he'd developed a genuine affection for his authors.

I look forward to seeing everyone again. Including the young lady who, after her third gin, exclaimed: 'It's such a pleasure talking to you, Mr Bunskin Ronde!'

Just call me Bun, dear.

Landour, Mussoorie
23 October 2001